Baited

Baited

Jennifer Dean

Little Fish Publishing
Seattle, Washington

ISBN: 978-1737303510

For Aunt Evie

CHAPTER 1

RISK

My hands gripped the steering wheel tightly as I looked out my windshield with a cautious stare. There was a calm stillness to the silence of my street that didn't carry through to my inner anxiety.

I lowered my forehead against my knuckles, closing my eyes as I released a heavy repressed sigh. After counting out my breaths, I slowly lifted my eyelids like a theatre curtain while my body pushed back in my seat. I shook my head, a small humorless grin occupying my lips as I began to digest what I had gotten myself into…

***

"What do I have to do?"

Jane smirked as if slightly impressed but she was barely able to open her mouth before she was interrupted.

"No," Sean said with sudden vehemence. "She isn't getting involved with this. Find another wa—"

"Don't you think if there was another way, she would have suggested it?"

My eyes shifted toward my brother but my neck remained firmly straightened toward Jane.

"Emma, I know you're still pissed at me but you have no idea what you're getting yourself into," Sean said.

"I never do when it comes to immortals."

Despite the coldness of my tone, I heard a few light chuckles around the room. My gaze shifted to the ground before I dared to look back up at the many bright, expectant eyes surrounding me.

"I know I can't do much, but I can do *this*."

"Are you sure?"

I turned back to Liam as I heard the concern in his voice. I imagined that if the roles were reversed, I would carry the same worry for him.

"Yes," I said, squeezing his hand to convey my assurance.

Once again, I turned my body to face Jane, bouncing my eyes up with a readied stare.

"What do I have to do?"

"I need you to know that what I'm asking comes with risk."

"I understand."

"No, you don't," Sean said. "By risk, she means you're willing to accept that this *help* may come at the cost of losing your life."

"He's right," Jane said. "I'm prepared to risk your life if it ultimately means bringing an end to Thomas."

"Well...at least you're honest," I said with uneasiness.

"I may be a bitch but at least I'm an honest one," Jane said.

It was hard to not find humor in her words, as if she were reading the tagline from a movie written about her.

"Look, as much as your presence annoys me, I don't wish to see your death. But I need you to know that this plan is about commitment. That goes for me as well. I'll need to play my part just as much as you will yours. At times, you may even question my loyalty. However, we must rely on trust because it's all we'll have until we see this through."

"So, you're saying it's going to get worse before it gets better."

It wasn't a question but a realization of the danger I was agreeing to dive into.

"Yes. This isn't going to be easy. He'll be seeking every opportunity for revenge for Liam's betrayal. A revenge that will create a blood trail straight to *you*. One that could lead to your death."

I caught sight of Mary's bright stare across the room. Her first words to me echoed in my mind. *Being with Liam means you will always be a target.*

I bit my lip with squinted eyes of confusion as I looked back at Jane. Before I could speak, my brother's outburst interrupted me.

"You want us to just sit back and leave her for him like some immortal bait?"

Sean's voice cracked with incredulity.

"He has to believe he has the upper hand. The only way that can happen is if you play your parts in leaving her vulnerable. From the moment I leave this house, you must portray a belief that the threat is gone."

"By leaving her to be killed!"

Jane closed her eyes in frustration before turning to face Sean. Her neck stiffened with impatience but she paused in speaking, as if waiting to gain the composure that one needed when speaking to a petulant child.

"Thomas is a sadistic prick who likes to play games. His immediate goal won't be to kill her but to show Liam and you that he *can* if he chooses to. You have to make it seem as if he's in control. Being overprotective isn't an option, Sean."

"I understand what you're saying and I even agree with your theory but as her brother, I can't just…"

Sean shook his head, clearly hoping to distract himself from the images circling his mind before turning a newly placed anger on Liam.

"You're ok with this?"

"Of course not," Liam said with an offended grimace. "I hate the idea of her being in any kind of harm's way. But she's going to do it whether I'm okay with this or not."

As Sean rolled his eyes, Liam continued with a small grin, as if the behavior only proved his point.

"You only disrespect her by not allowing her to make this choice. So, regardless of your inability to accept it, I'll stand by whatever *she* decides."

"Thank you," I said.

It was all I had time to say before a thud caused me to snap my neck back around. Sean stood facing the wall with his palms flat against it. He refused to look at anyone behind him. My eyes traveled up to a spot near his left hand, where I saw a deep hole the size of his fist.

The tension in the room lingered as I met his gaze. I had barely blinked before he moved to a kneeling position in front of me, his hands reaching out to hold mine with comforting warmth.

"Please don't do this. I know you hate me and that's fine. Hate me all you want. But please don't make me have to risk your life this way. You don't have to do this."

I looked into his pleading eyes, knowing that even with my anger I could never hate him. I paused, squeezing his fingers without breaking his bright golden gaze. "No, I don't *have* to do this but I *want* to do this."

He lowered his head in defeat before rising back to his feet and turning his attention to Jane. He remained silent, his body tense as he resignedly stood and walked back toward Grace.

"I'm short on time so I must leave you all," Jane said. Then she looked at me. "I hope you survive this, Emma, I really do. But if fate has other plans, please know your sacrifice will have been an honorable one."

"Thank you," I said.

I reached for Liam's hand as Jane nodded with appreciation before she looked toward the leader of the Alexanders. Patrick gave one subtle nod of approval. It was enough verbal communication for Jane to begin walking backward in farewell.

"Good luck."

As soon as Jane left the Alexander Mansion, each immortal remaining in the room took a moment to pass by me with a gentle squeeze of affection before heading off in their own direction— all except Sean, who seemed to have already slipped out of the house without notice before Jane's exit.

I swung my legs up on the couch and leaned back into Liam's chest. I sighed, causing him to wrap his warm arms around me and place a soft kiss on my temple.

My eyes closed as if exhausted by the heavy deal I had just made. I hoped, for the sake of the one who held me and the one who had stormed off minutes ago, that I would make it out of this alive.

***

I shook the thoughts out of my head as I reached my hand down to pop the trunk of my car. Preparing for Thomas to make his move was like being forced to sit cross-legged in front of a hissing cobra and waiting for the inevitable bite.

But I still had to remain calm—on the outside at least. Life had to be as normal as it possibly could. The plan depended on it.

I smiled and shook my head with the absurdity that had come to my life in the past year. I was still shaking my head at the thought as I stepped out into the chilly air and made my way to the back of my car.

It was a bit odd to pick up a few things for my own birthday party but I was grateful for the distraction. I was reaching down to grab more of the bags when I felt a presence behind me.

"Can I carry those for you?" Liam asked.

I turned around to find a smile that matched my own. With the groceries momentarily forgotten, I began to walk toward him.

"I didn't think I'd be seeing you for a while," I said.

"I missed that smile of yours too much."

I couldn't hide my impatient longing as I took his outstretched hand, which eagerly pulled my body into his own. But despite Liam's ability to hold his breath for an infinite amount of time, he still seemed quite breathless once we finally pulled away from our kiss.

I brought my hand up to gently caress his cheek, watching as he closed his eyes and leaned gratefully into my touch.

"I love you," I said.

Upon my words, Liam's eyes opened to reveal the subtle wetness that had been present for days. It was a sight he kept hidden from anyone who wasn't me. But it was quite amazing how the very gaze of the same emerald green glow sent a tightness to my stomach.

He grinned before lifting his hand to let his thumb trace my lips. He then leaned down to lay his forehead against mine.

"I love you too."

Unable to resist, I pressed my lips against his, wrapping my hands around his neck. Feeling his protective hold around my back only sped up my passionate urge but I reluctantly pulled back, knowing we should move into the house to prevent prying eyes from seeing us. Liam chuckled at the slight moan I made upon parting from his lips. I joined in with his amusement with my own giggle as he kissed my temple.

We let go of one another briefly so that Liam could swiftly grab all four bags with one hand, leaving his other free to hold mine. I entwined my fingers with his and leaned against his arm while contemplating my choice from over a year ago.

I merely smiled as we walked toward the house, knowing that loving Liam was not wise or easy but was certainly worth the risk.

CHAPTER 2

LAST DESCENDANT

It took several blinks before I was able to focus on the low light around my room. My head turned toward the movement on my left, where Liam lay propped against his elbow. I couldn't help but roll to my side in excitement at the warm grin upon his lips.

"Happy birthday," Liam said softly in my ear.

He laid his hand on my cheek. It felt as if the blood beneath my skin followed his touch like a magnet.

"It is, isn't it?"

Liam's grin widened, causing mine to do the same "Sean and I are the same age," I said with a sly smile, knowing that Sean would be listening to the thought. I could even see him attempting to not roll his eyes at the very sentence.

I pressed into Liam's firm and chiseled immortal body, feeling it mold around my own as if we were perfect puzzle pieces reunited.

I laid back, enjoying the fleeting moment with Liam as I remembered the promise I had made to spend time alone with my mom this afternoon.

"Wait," I said, feeling my bladder calling me. "I'll be right back."

Liam chuckled as I hopped off the bed and headed for the bathroom to relieve my bladder and brush my teeth. A new chuckle came to my lips as I opened my door to the sight of the new block lettered poster my mom had left on my bedroom door. It seemed this year she had added a few more balloons above the large written number.

"Did you hear her putting this up this morning?"

Liam tried to resist a smirk as he nodded in confirmation. I shook my head as I walked into the bathroom. When I came back out, I saw Liam standing at the edge of my bed. The perfect fit of his navy-blue sweater involuntarily made me lick my bottom lip.

Oddly enough, it seemed he was having his own trouble keeping his eyes off my legs, left bare by my pajama shorts. I felt the warmth of my blush but held a small satisfaction at knowing that I wasn't the only one affected. My attention was soon brought to the large wrapped package he held in front of him.

"What is that?"

"I have your birthday gift," Liam said.

My eyebrows lifted as I stepped closer and bent down so that I was eye level with the gift. I reached around the back, gaining a good grip that let me rip the paper all the way around the front to carefully reveal a canvas painting.

"Wow," I said.

My concentrated voice was low as I studied the detailed portrait of my face pressed gently against Liam's chest. Even in a fictional portrayal, Liam had captured the perfect likeness of his own gaze of protective admiration. The detail in his work left me breathless.

"Do you like it?"

Once again, he had lowered his wall, letting in the small vulnerability that carried a self-conscious tone.

"Liam, it's beautiful. I love it."

His smile was angelic with modesty as I stood back up to embrace his lips passionately. "It's the best gift I've ever gotten. Thank you."

"You're welcome."

I paused, looking down at his hands to hide my insecurity.

"Do you have to leave soon?"

"Yes," Liam said while lifting my chin with a gentle nudge from his fingertips.

I nodded, taking his hand. He began to lead us toward the window. My smile seemed to deflate along with my body upon knowing that I had to part with him. Of course, a large part of that had more to do with the fact that my heart still felt a twinge upon any goodbyes the past couple of days held with him.

I watched the reluctance in Liam's eyes as he focused on the window, lifting it without the need of a touch from either one of us.

"I'll see you at the party later?

He studied my face, trying to resist a new chuckle.

"Of course."

I raised my eyebrows, twitching them dramatically.

"Sounds good."

My voice was level but my heart raced, as I knew it was time for him to go. Sensing my unease, Liam moved his right hand to my cheek while his left rested upon my waist, pulling me closer. My hands slid up to rest flat upon his chest just before his other hand rose to my cheek. He held my face within his grasp for a second before placing his lips down to mine.

In those seconds, it was easy to let go of my fear—at least until he pulled away, leaving me breathless and terrified once more.

"I'll see you soon," he said as if it were a scared promise.

"Okay," I said with a low breath, never looking away from his eyes. I tried desperately to hide the light gulp that came from my throat but Liam heard it like an echo.

"What is it?"

I attempted to look down but he pulled up my chin to stare into his eyes, almost making me forget my fear.

"Sometimes I can't help but think that you're going to ripple and disappear from me." I shook my head as if embarrassed by the spoken words. "Like this is all just…a cruel dream."

I closed my eyes to the memory of the times I stood in my room, wishing for him to hold me. But instead *that* Liam would only ripple away, leaving me with a withered petal each time he left me behind.

Suddenly he leaned back down to kiss me fiercely, as if to show his solidness. I wrapped my arms around him, feeling an escaped tear sliding down my cheek. It was an odd happiness that had seemed impossible the past few months.

As he pulled away, he used his thumbs to softly wipe the wetness from my face.

"I saw you too," Liam admitted.

"You did?"

"Every night after our last phone call," he said through a small nod. "When you showed in the clearing, it took me a minute to realize that you were real. And even though every part of my body longed for you, I had hoped you would disappear like all the other times because I didn't want you in that danger. I couldn't bear it if I had to watch you…"

Our emotions were raw and exposed, yet safe in the room where they lingered between us.

"My stomach still won't unclench. It's like it still believes this is all a lie and wants to protect me when you disappear again."

He pulled my face up so that it was only inches from his lips, as if to help me see that his face was real.

"I'm here," he whispered.

I smiled, remembering my transparent Liam's exact words on the day of my dad's funeral.

"I can't almost lose you like that again. I know that I wouldn't survive it."

With a contented sigh, I laid my head against his chest. I felt his cheek rest atop my head with his own solace.

"Nor would I, love," he said with a low sigh into my hair.

The peaceful comfort was enough for us to pull away in unison and allow him to finally leave. I walked forward, following his exit as he backed out of the window agilely. When my feet could go no farther, he placed his right hand to my face for a moment before dropping it and running off into the distance.

I stood in my place for a couple of seconds until the cold air caused me to stiffen. Quickly, I shut the window, letting in the air that lingered with Liam's scent before finally heading back to the bathroom.

After my shower, I found my stereo remote next to my jeans. I quickly shuffled through the channels until I found a fast-beat song. I slipped on my jeans with ease before grabbing a plaid tunic blouse. While dancing around the room, I smiled at the thought of Liam learning of the goofy mood I was in mere seconds after he left me.

I was holding my locket with one hand and a book in the other when my mother called for me.

"Emma!"

As I turned the corner from the hallway, I saw my mom setting down a white, two-layer fondant cake with beautiful handmade purple icing flowers surrounding it. It amazed me at times how the talent of somebody's hobby could outshine their occupation.

Looking around, I saw that the entire living room was decorated with a sleek and creative theme of purple and black. Standing next to one of the purple-draped tables was my uncle, who was beaming at my entrance.

Out of habit, I looked around for my dad only to feel the harsh reminder that he was missing. Moments like that reminded me that it would probably take years for the habit to go away.

Without really thinking, I turned back to the living room, grabbed the remote, and turned the TV onto ESPN. Today was not a day I wanted to think about my father's death. Having ESPN in the background was a crutch I used to distract myself.

When I re-entered the kitchen, my uncle followed with a sympathetic smile, while my mom gave a nod of approval and understanding.

"You're here early," I teased him.

"I know but I figured I'd beat the crowd."

"Right," I said as I saw him grab a small purple bag stuffed with lavender tissue paper.

"I got you a little something," he said, moving forward with an infectious smile to hand me the gift.

I side-glanced at my mom, who was smiling sweetly at his words, as she finished placing more tiny flowers onto this year's cake. I had to admit, I loved how much it seemed to help my mother to have my uncle around. But then again, it always had.

Focusing back on the bag, I reached in to pull out a small sparklingly white replica of the Eifel tower. Looking up to see my uncle's large grin, I knew there was something else. I reached back inside to find a thin white and blue envelope. I opened the packet to find two open-ended first-class tickets to Paris, France.

My smile dropped as my eyebrows lifted in shock. I looked up to see the shifted grin of my uncle. Though still genuine, it wasn't quite of the same playful nature it had been moments before.

"Are these real?" I asked, holding up the tickets.

"Yep."

"How? No, wait…why?"

I couldn't quite get my thoughts around this generosity.

"I know it's been a hard couple of months with your boyfriend moving away and then losing your dad, Emma."

I looked down, an awkward feeling arising until I heard his voice break it.

"I just wanted you to be able to go somewhere after you graduate. To be able to get away from reality before college." He paused, reaching out to playfully shove me. "You used to talk about Paris all the time so I thought it would be a good place to send you."

I looked back at him but out of the corner of my eye, I could see that my mom was staring at us.

"But I don't deserve a free trip to Paris. You do," I said, gesturing in my mom's direction.

She put down her utensils, which told me she was about to speak her piece. I was not one to interrupt her. Not in this moment.

"Baby, life is cruel and I've had time to accept that lesson. But losing a parent so young, you've lost a piece of your innocence."

She looked over at my uncle meaningfully. He looked back at her with synced approval.

"We want you to have this time to forget. You don't realize how much you deserve yourself, sweetheart."

I was speechless for a moment, looking back and forth between them. If only I could tell them how much the gift meant to me but that I was almost certain I would never get the chance to use it. That we should cherish this birthday because it might be my last. But instead, I merely rose my chin and said, "Thank you."

My mom, who misread the reason for my emotion, had come over to pull me into a hug. I turned to my uncle, who waited patiently, and closed both arms around him.

"Happy birthday, kid."

"Thanks," I said while pulling back out of a desperate need for space. "I'm going to go put it in a safe place."

"Oh, Em?" my mom said.

"Yeah?" I said, turning back around.

"I was going to visit your dad's grave this weekend with your uncle. Do you want to come with us?"

If I had looked awkward before, I'm sure it was nothing compared to my next stumble.

"Um…that's…that's alright. I'll go another time."

"Okay, sweetie."

I couldn't understand why I was unable to handle the simplicity of visiting my dad's grave but I knew that was her way of telling me there was no rush.

Once I came back from my room, I had barely turned the corner before my mother's eagerness rose to the surface.

"Ok babe, now my gift."

I walked over to the open seat that my mom had left me between Uncle Greg and herself. On the glass table sat a thick black box with a little red bow on top. I reached down to grab the box and pull it to my lap, where I slowly opened it to reveal a thin silver bracelet with several engraved fleur-de-lis markings.

"It has been passed down to different generations in the Morgan family."

"Really," I said, inspecting it delicately with my fingers.

"Yes, it goes all the way back to your French ancestor, Jacques Bastien, who created the bracelet for his daughter on her wedding day so that she would always remember where she came from."

I looked up in awe as I sensed her pause for composure.

"The family tradition has always been for the father to give this to his oldest daughter when she reaches eighteen."

I looked down to trace the French carvings that looped into the two small B's representing the surname of my ancestors.

Upon hearing her strained voice, I looked back to see her dropped shoulders of disappointment.

"Your father was really excited to finally be able to give this to you."

My free hand moved to grip hers with comfort. She looked down with a grin as if my very touch brought her strength.

"Your grandparents never had any girls so the bracelet moved on to the next generation."

I turned to my uncle and held the bracelet out to him. "Would you put it on for me?"

"I'd be honored," he said, turning to take the bracelet from the box in my hands.

I laid the empty box back down to my lap and held out my left wrist. Once he had clasped the chain, I stared at the antique reminder that was around the wrist of its last descendant.

CHAPTER 3

First and Last

"Happy birthday," four voices said in unison.

"Thanks," I said while stepping aside to let my friends in the door.

"Hi girls," my mom said as she came out of the kitchen with my uncle. "You can put your gifts over here."

Lauren followed my mom while the three other girls trailed behind her.

"Oh wow. Awesome cake," Becca said.

I silently shook my head in amusement as I began to shut the door—at least until I caught sight of four more people walking up the porch. It was the Harris family plus Matt's fiancée,

Paige, who I couldn't help but notice had a confident glow about her as her eyes met mine.

"Matt and I were still on holiday break so I hope you don't mind us crashing another one of your parties," Paige said.

"Don't be silly." My hand waved forward to dismiss her acknowledgment of intrusion. "The more people to help finish that cake, the better," I said while gesturing my thumb behind me.

"I'm game," Michael said.

"Of course you are," I said, rolling my eyes before shifting them back up to look between James, Matt, and Paige. "Come on in."

"Happy birthday," James said while tenderly holding my shoulder for a brief moment.

"Thank you," I responded, not quite meeting his eyes. I knew the pity they would be carrying and I wasn't quite ready to dive into the events that had gone down at Thanksgiving. Instead, I turned to face Paige's readied interest.

"Have you guys set a date yet?"

Her cheeks rose with a beaming smile that couldn't possibly show any more teeth.

"March third," she said while pausing with the hopeful lift of her eyebrows. "I hope you'll be able to come."

"Wouldn't miss it," I said, shutting the door behind them.

She smiled as Matt led her farther into the living room. After James headed toward my uncle, I turned back to Michael, who had yet to move.

"Do you want a drink?"

"Sure."

"Follow me then," I said.

"You're the boss."

I elbowed him lightly in the ribs as I caught Pamela and Becca's playful stares. "Shut up and come on."

As we walked toward the kitchen, I shook my head subtly, as if that would help rid me of the sudden false memory that flew into my mind: of Michael's lips against mine. Every time it reappeared, it felt like waking up from a dream and struggling to reach the surface of my own reality—a reality that always left him ignorant and me standing next to him with awkward embarrassment.

"Root beer or tea?"

"Root beer, please."

Just as I turned to hand him a bottle, I took notice of the blue box behind his back.

"I'm sorry. I should have told you that you could put that with the others on the table."

"Oh, I saw them but I wanted to give it to you myself."

"Oh," I said, surprised. "Can I open it now?"

"It's *your* birthday," Michael said while placing the gift into my hands.

I swiftly ripped off the wrapping paper to reveal a plain white box. Seeing the two pieces of tape, I sat it on the table and pulled at the pieces until the box was free to lift, revealing the same blue color of tissue paper. I parted it to find a wooden frame with a picture inside.

"Oh my god, is this…"

"Yeah. That's us."

I picked up the frame to get a closer look at the two small children giggling as they played with chalk, unaware of the lens that was capturing their moment.

"My mom took that picture the summer before we started kindergarten."

"I remember we used to play with this stuff for hours," I said with a small exhale of laughter.

"I know it's not much. But…"

"Yes, it is," I said. "There is so much sentiment in this gift. I love it. Thank you."

I leaned in to quickly peck his cheek before reaching around to gather the torn paper in my hands. As I made my way to the trash can, I heard him clear his throat slightly.

"So…where's Sean?"

I could hear the slight stutter as if he'd been about to say something else but changed his mind. I shut the pantry door and sighed before walking back toward him.

"He couldn't get out of work."

I always hated this part. Maybe a little part of me resented the old days when I was ignorant of what he was. Before *I* had to be the one to come up with the excuse.

"That sucks."

"Tell me about it," I said bitterly before pressing the tissue paper back down and grabbing the top of the box.

"Hey, Emma?"

"Yeah," I said while turning to lean back against the island. It was then that I noticed his eyes weren't looking at me but at the kitchen table, which he was running one of his fingers over.

"Well, I know it's months away but I was wondering if you maybe wanted to go to prom together this year?"

My eyebrows rose and my mouth opened slightly as his baby blue eyes finally met mine.

"Oh...um...I..."

His brow furrowed at my stutter. Suddenly I wasn't so sure what his mind had been changed back to. My mind swarmed with panic but my face remained still.

As far as I knew, everyone—including Michael—thought Liam had broken up with me after his family moved back to Oregon. No one was aware they were back or that I had been grieving his death.

I was internally asking myself if this was Michael organically asking as a supportive friend or because he was attempting something more. Unfortunately, the way he was unable to meet my gaze following the original question told me it was probably the latter.

My mouth began to dry as the true awkwardness of the moment crept into my veins.

"Here you are."

I turned to Liam's grinning face, breathing out relief as our gazes locked on to one another.

"Hi," I said.

"Hey," Liam said with a wink.

"What's *he* doing here?"

My trance was broken as Michael spoke, forcing me to look back over and notice that the fidgeting shyness had been replaced with a strained tension in his fists.

"He moved back over the break."

I was still looking at Michael when Liam wrapped his arm around my waist and leaned in to kiss my temple. He wasn't boasting, just sensing that the tension needed to be eased.

"Happy birthday."

"Thank you," I said with giddiness. "Even though you already told me this morning."

He chuckled.

"Oh. *Oh*. You're back together?" Michael said with a small twitch of his upper lip.

"Yes," I said.

"So quickly after what he did?"

Michael's grimace had gone from subtle to a clear disdain that he could no longer hide.

"It's complicated."

Michael sighed. I feared that he would lecture me with a cliché response but instead, he bounced his glare up to meet Liam.

"If you hurt her again, I'll kick your ass," Michael said.

Liam's brow rose at the unexpected threat. "Fair enough."

With that, Michael turned to walk out of the kitchen. He continued over to his brother and whispered something in his ear before making a subtle exit out the front door.

The guilt made my stomach tense as I walked back over to Liam. I wrapped both arms around him and felt his gentle kiss on the top of my head.

"I always liked him," Liam said.

I chuckled. "Me too."

After the last guest had left the party, Liam and I began helping my mom and uncle clean, only to have them refuse the help.

"I don't mind helping."

She shook her head. "No baby, it's your birthday. We've got this."

"Mrs. Morgan, would you mind if I stole Emma for the rest of the night?"

She was doing her best to hide her grin. "Of course not. Go have fun."

"Thank you," Liam said as he took my hand and guided me out the front door.

Getting in his car, I felt relieved to be alone with him for the first time since this morning. As I looked up at his face, it appeared that his lifted cheekbones showed that he carried the same thought.

"What did you need to steal me for?"

"I have a surprise for you," Liam said.

"You do?"

I began to think of what else he could have for me. It was then that I noticed we had pulled up to the curved drive of the Alexander Mansion.

Once I was out of the car, he swept me off the ground in a bridal hold. I closed my eyes as I turned into his chest for warmth, preparing to move at immortal speed. It took me only one time to realize that having them open when he ran would cause my human body to need 20 minutes to recover.

"Open," Liam said seconds later as he placed me on the ground.

I took in the beautiful warmth of a new sight. There in front of us was a large willow tree with a handmade layout of lavender, white lilies, and roses on the ground. Stepping closer, I heard the light voice of Billie Holiday, which grew louder as we approached. In amazement, I looked back over to the willow tree to study the fairy style of twinkling lights beaming with a perfect glow.

I looked at Liam, who held a small grin of pleasure upon seeing my reaction to his surprise. He then bowed before extending his hand to mine. I took it without hesitation. He spun me in a twirl that pulled me close until we were swaying to each of his leading movements.

"Happy birthday, Emma."

It felt fitting that he was the first and last person I saw on my birthday. And as he leaned in to kiss me tenderly, leaving a trickle on my lips, I knew that no other birthday would be able to compare. But I hoped we'd made it out of Jane's plan so that he could prove me wrong.

CHAPTER 4

SPACE

It was the first time in months that I felt as if I were walking the school hallways without a constant heavy fog looming over me. But it didn't go unnoticed. When the veil of my unhappiness lifted, the curiosity of those around me surfaced.

And if I thought my birthday party had been awkward, it didn't compare to Liam's reappearance at the lunch table. Not that I could blame them. His sudden place by my side was bound to raise questions among everyone who expected to never see him again.

But that didn't make the first few seconds of silence any easier. This was why I found myself grateful for Becca's boldness in jumping in and breaking it—even if it was for her own selfish curiosity.

"So Liam, how was Oregon?" Becca asked.

Pamela gleefully looked up while resting her hand near her jawbone. Erika pretended to strike up a conversation with Jen Adams about homework, while Lauren briefly closed her eyes with a small embarrassed shake of her head. Michael simply kept eating, as if the topic bored him.

Liam squeezed my hand under the table, sensing my need for comfort. But to others, it appeared as if he merely grinned politely, twitching his lips in amusement at the question.

"It was harder than expected."

Though he was answering the entire table, he looked directly at Becca as he spoke.

"I doubt you had it harder than Emma."

I was as surprised as everyone else to hear Michael's acidic tone next to me.

"Michael," I said with a warning of caution.

Michael was staring at Liam, his hands clenched on his tray as if resisting the urge to throw it. But if he was expecting a reaction, he was left empty-handed. Liam merely gave a well-composed nod.

"I never said that I did," Liam said.

My stomach clenched at the familiar awkwardness arising from the identical one-sided glare that Sean held every time Liam had been near me last year.

I gently punched Michael in the arm to gain his attention. Only then did he seem to snap out of his anger and shift his eyes back to me. As I looked at his baby blue gaze, I found that his eyes were full of unexpected regret.

"I'm sorry," Michael said.

My cheeks felt flushed, embarrassed by the eyes of the entire table.

"I've been stressed lately…" He paused, shaking his head in a shameful way that beckoned me to pat his arm

I noticed Pamela's lifted brow as her eyes shifted toward Becca, who mouthed the words, "clearly."

"I didn't mean to take it out on you," Michael said with his eyes on Liam.

"It's okay."

With a heavy mental sigh, I watched Michael accept Liam's forgiveness before looking back over at my immortal boyfriend's grin. A chill of excitement shot into my stomach like a cocoon that had burst open with a thousand butterflies. The thrill of watching Liam's admiration for me always took me by surprise— in the best way.

But my attention was stolen again when I turned to the sound of Michael abruptly standing with his tray.

"Where are you going?" I asked.

He didn't look at me, only his tray, as he responded to my confusion.

"I need to see Coach Mackey."

I had barely opened my mouth before he had moved, quickly making his way to the trash and out the door to find the baseball coach.

I looked back at Liam, knowing he would read the worried expression on my face. But I shrugged as if to convey I would ask about what was *stressing* Michael later. Liam nodded before teasingly grabbing the uneaten cookie off my tray.

With my eyes still watchfully on him, I knew Liam wouldn't take the chance of actually taking a bite. But my uneven smirk dared him to expose the heightened glow of his emerald eyes that would always come from ingesting any food substance.

Instead, he relented with a wink before putting the cookie back, knowing quite well I would revel in the small victory.

Hours later, when I pulled into the parking lot of Morgan Therapy, I didn't see the blue truck anywhere. There was only an unfamiliar green Explorer parked near Michael's usual spot.

My disappointment expanded as I walked inside to find a blond boy in his mid-twenties sitting at the front desk. He smiled at my entrance as if expecting me.

"You must be Emma. I'm David."

I smiled politely as I inched closer to where he sat. Then I slowly lifted my arm to shake his extended hand.

"Hi, David. Is Michael not working today?"

"Michael Harris?"

"That's the one," I said with a tight-lipped grin.

While my tone bore no amusement, he laughed back flirtatiously.

"He quit."

I moved my head back in shock. "He quit?"

"Yup," David said nodding with a smile I didn't appreciate.

"Do you know why?"

"Sorry, no."

"Is my uncle in the back?"

"He's in his office."

"Thanks," I said, moving without another word. I took a long breath before stepping into the open door of my uncle's office. At the sight of me, his cheeks lifted along with his eyes.

"Hey kid," he said as he looked back down at a file he was reviewing

"Hey," I said before diving into my inquiry. "Did Michael quit?"

"Well, yeah. Didn't he tell you?"

"No," I said, ignoring the vulnerability of being the last to know. My uncle eyed me incredulously.

"He's seemed stressed lately at school but I haven't been able to talk to him about it. Did he say why?"

My uncle looked back up, his eyebrows raised in concern.

"Well, I always knew he was going to stop working here once the season started..." My uncle paused, bobbing his head while his eyes shifted back and forth as if contemplating a problem. "But a few days ago, he asked if I could let him loose earlier than planned."

My nod mirrored his own as memories circled in my mind.

"Hmm," I said in contemplation. "He did mention needing to see Coach Mackey at lunch today. Do you think he's been stressed about his position?"

"Well kid, my guess is that he's feeling the pressure from preparing for college scouts."

"Right," I said.

I nodded at the realization. *College.* I mean, that was what most seniors were supposed to be worrying about, right? How stupid to not be aware of the reality, even if it differed from my own.

My uncle smiled up at me before looking back at another file. It was as if he knew I had reached the correct conclusion and his guidance was no longer needed.

"Later kid," he said with amusement as he watched me back out of his office.

"See ya," I said while walking down the hallway. By the time I got back to the lobby, I knew it would be rude to ignore David, even if I was eager to escape his unwanted flirtation.

"Nice meeting you," I said without carrying the actual meaning behind the words. Unfortunately, my fake politeness came off too well.

"Oh, you're not staying?"

David's features betrayed a slight disappointment that I was all too ready to leave behind.

"Nope," I said, not caring to expand on the reason as I pushed open the door.

Suddenly, I was met with a cold breeze that stung my skin with a bitterness. It was as if I'd been too distracted before to take notice of the weather but now I was all too grateful to find sanctuary in my car.

I started the engine, following my need as it led me to the Harris driveway. I had knocked only once before it swung open. James, who must have been in the living room, stood on the other side with a smile that would make even an enemy feel welcome.

"Hey, Emma. It's been a while."

"I know, I'm sorry."

He shook his head with a small wave of his hand to dismiss my apology.

"That's okay." He paused, opening his mouth and sticking out his chin. At least that was until he seemed to suddenly talk himself out of any more words.

Honestly, I was grateful he had stopped himself from diving into the need to acknowledge my father's death again. I had come to realize over the past month that hearing someone's sympathy never made me feel any better. It merely created an awkward atmosphere for me and them.

"Michael's in his room."

James stood aside, gesturing his hand in several forward movements.

"Thanks."

It didn't take long to find the last bedroom on the right side of the house. I lightly tapped on the door. It felt odd to see it closed.

"Come in."

I stiffened, caught off guard by the hard, risen voice. It wasn't acidic or annoyed, just distracted, as if he were ready for the person on the other side of the door to state their business and leave. Cautiously, I opened the door to find Michael sitting at the small desk at the far end of his square room. As I walked through the frame, he turned, his eyebrows rising in surprise at my presence.

"Oh, hey," Michael said with a tight line forming on his mouth. He looked back down at the notebook on his desk.

My eyes narrowed and my chin lowered in annoyance at what came across as a dismissal.

"That's all I get?"

"What do you mean?"

"I mean…" I pointed my hand toward his face. "You look like Heather just walked into your room."

"Don't even joke about such things. It's not like that thought hasn't crossed her mind."

"Well…at this point it feels like she'd get a better greeting than I would."

He chuckled but it was an odd sound that felt as if he were simply placating me.

"So, why are you here?"

My head pulled back. I was becoming more annoyed that he wasn't even looking at me while he spoke with a bored tone.

"I came to see what the hell is wrong with my friend…but I'm not sure if he's here."

He sighed, his eyes shifting up while the left side of his mouth seemed to twitch with humor at something I had said.

"What makes you think something's wrong?"

I rolled my eyes, feeling the air coming harshly out of my nose as I made my way to sit at the edge of his bed.

"Because we haven't talked much since my birthday party," I said, watching as his gaze finally met mine fully. "And then what happened at lunch today…"

He remained quiet, seeming to bite his inner cheek while looking to his left, desperate to avoid the oncoming confrontation.

"Were you even going to tell me that you quit? It was kind of awkward walking in to find some random guy at the desk." I paused to make a side note. "And by the way, he came off a little creepy."

I smiled victoriously once Michael could no longer hold his laughter.

"Not a fan of David?"

"Let's just say I don't see myself going in there to visit my uncle unless I need to."

Finally, the Michael I knew seemed to take back control as he stood and moved to sit beside me on his bed, unable to resist the toothy grin that escaped. I teasingly bumped his shoulder with mine.

"Seriously, why didn't you tell me? I felt like I was the last to know."

"Sorry…this past week has just been hard for me."

"Does it have to do with baseball or deciding on where you want to go—"

"No," Michael said, interrupting me while looking at his hands.

"Oh," I said, confused. "Then what is it?"

"It's nothing."

"It's obviously *something*. So, if it's not baseball, what is it?"

"Just drop it, Emma, okay?"

He stood so quickly that the bounce of the bed almost threw me off, yet I was unwilling to give up. I rose to my feet, looking at him with an unrelenting stare.

"No, not until you tell me what's wrong. And this..." I paused to gesture in a hard, wavy direction toward him. "Only proves my point."

He still wasn't looking at me, his eyes only moving toward the ground. Feeling frustrated, I pulled at his arm.

"Michael," I pleaded. "What's wrong with you?"

My voice had risen unintentionally but it was enough to get him to finally look up at me, though it appeared to be involuntary.

"I'm sorry," he whispered. "Really, Emma, I'm sorry if I'm being a jerk. It's just..." He closed his eyes for a moment before throwing his head back in frustration. "It's just hard to be around you."

"What?"

I dropped his arm, my head pulling back. I knew I was unable to keep the hurt from flooding into my eyes. But his silence only agitated me.

"Why now? Is this about Liam? I know you don't think I should have taken him back but—"

"That's not it," he said shaking his head as if he were trapped in his own disbelief.

"Then what is it? Why can't you be around me?"

His jaw tensed and his lips pulled inward as if he were battling his inner thoughts. It was hard to tell who was going to win out when he suddenly spoke.

"Because I'm in love with you. I'm in love with you and you're in love with someone else."

Instinctively I stepped back, my mouth open but no words came out. Michael studied my face, his eyes carrying both sympathy and fear.

"See, this is why I wanted you to just drop it..." He paused, his frustration leading him to pace.

"Michael..."

He walked back over, leaving a few inches between us.

"I know I should have said something before now...before he came back. But I finally got the courage to say something at your birthday and then..."

"You found out Liam was back," I said.

"Yeah," Michael said. "Something like that."

"But why does that mean we can't still hang out like before? We were always able to...even while Liam and I were together."

"It's different."

My eyes dropped to the ground, matching the defeat in my shoulders. My mind swam within the real memory I had repressed of Michael trying to kiss me on the day of my father's funeral. But the repressed memory for me was merely feelings lingering beneath the surface for Michael. And it seemed that now that Liam had returned, those feelings had broken free.

Shit, I thought, unable to convey any other words. I began to open my mouth but stopped, knowing that any plea would feel selfish. Of course, that didn't mean Michael didn't feel the disappointment of my silence.

"I just can't right now, Emma. Being around you reminds me of what I can never have. So for now, I just need some distance. And if you care for me at all—"

"You know that I do," I interrupted.

"Then you'll give me that." His voice was barely a whisper. "Please."

"Okay," I said with a small nod.

I didn't hesitate to make my exit, not even stopping to turn back with a smile or goodbye wave. He needed distance from me in order to accept that he and I would never be an option. If the tables had been turned, I would probably make the same request.

As I walked toward my car, I contemplated the timing of it all. I let out a sardonic chuckle. Maybe it was good. And perhaps considering the looming threat surrounding me, it was a space I needed to keep for myself too.

CHAPTER 5

REASON 146

I walked with Lauren out the front doors. When we reached the parking lot, I mumbled a curse under my breath—one that I was certain hadn't been as silent as I'd intended. But what I loved about Lauren was her observant sense that combined itself with a compassionate nature. It was a quality she remained firmly attached to as she followed my gaze a few cars down to find Michael talking to his long-time best friend, Travis.

Even after three weeks of cold turkey avoidance, my instinct was still to wave. But my arms remained at my sides, fidgeting in protest until my gaze was met by a pair of uninviting eyes.

I should have been grateful that the stare belonged to Travis and not Michael. At least I told myself that I *should* be grateful.

Instead, I found myself defensive about the unfriendly manner. I knew it wasn't Michael's fault that his friend was suddenly averse to me but it still felt as if he were unintentionally recruiting others to his side. Even the lunch table found itself scrambling with different daily arrangements.

Despite my better judgment, my hand released itself with a wave. I watched as the gesture caught Michael's attention. His lips remained still and his eyebrows rose in acknowledgment as if I were an unfamiliar acquaintance who had approached him in the hallway. I could see the mannerism fooling most into being perceived as polite but I knew instantly that it was fake. I did my best to match it but I didn't feel my effort was as good as his.

"I'll see you tomorrow."

I turned, grateful that the sound of Lauren's voice brought me out of the absorbed moment. I ignored the sympathy lingering in her eyes as I nodded with a small grin that dropped within seconds.

"Yeah, see you tomorrow."

I waited until I was in my car to close my eyes and release a deep sigh. I tried to remind myself that I had larger issues to worry about—bigger than the guilt that seemed to be dragging me down. It was a guilt that corrupted my brain with the false memories we shared. A guilt that grew as the memories swam in my brain. Seeing Michael only agitated them into haunting me.

"Stop," I whispered while pressing the palms of my hands against my temples.

I shook my head, letting my mind drift to the only image that would both calm my mind and set my soul on fire. Only when the emerald glow deep within my mind surfaced was I able to open my eyes again and focus.

I started my engine with a smile as I thought about the one person who would hold the inviting stare I always craved—the very same one I spotted leaning against the back of his BMW, dressed in a pair of dark-washed jeans and a thin layered t-shirt. It was oddly warm for February but not *that* warm.

And yet I had to bit my lip at the sight of his exposed arms as I stepped out from my car.

"Hi," I said, walking closer.

I could feel the blush warm my cheeks as I walked into his reached-out arms.

"Hi," Liam said

"I missed you."

He immediately leaned down to place his lips on mine, embracing the passion we both had been suppressing all day. A small moan made its way out of my throat without much control as he pulled back enough to lean his forehead against mine. He didn't need words to convey that he also loathed when we were apart.

"I hate when your Watch is during school hours."

He kissed my temple before looking back at me with an angelic smile.

"Let me make it up to you."

My eyebrows rose in intrigue as he led me by the hand to the passenger door. After my acceptance, it seemed as if time had barely passed before he was leading me up the stairs of the

Alexander Mansion. I expected to continue on toward his room but suddenly we made a sharp turn to the right.

"Where are we going?"

I looked up but he remained silent. By the way his cheeks pulled up, I could tell he was up to something. I had opened my mouth to ask again only to remain standing in silent confusion as we stopped in front of the bathroom door.

At first, I had found it funny that the Alexanders designed their houses with bathrooms. It wasn't as if hygiene was ever an issue. But it didn't take long for me to realize—and with much teasing from Lillian—that immortals found other ways to indulge. It was not much different from knowing that Liam's bed was used far less for sleep than for *other* things.

Liam moved to stand behind me, lowering his lips to my ear.

"Close your eyes," he said.

"Okay," I said eagerly.

I waited with blind anticipation, feeling Liam lead me forward.

"Open," he whispered.

I blinked my eyes open, ready for the surprise waiting for me. My mouth remained open in shock as my gaze bounced around the room. The floor was lined with petals and the air was enchanted with a mixture of clean linen and lavender. The large roman tub was filled with water that held a slight pink glow.

I turned around, unable to hold back my blissful smile.

"Did you do this?"

"I had Grace prepare it while I went to pick you up," Liam said.

I stepped forward until I was close enough to place my lips on his. Once I pulled back, he lifted his hand to caress my cheek with deep longing magnetized beneath his touch.

"Does this make up for not getting to see you all day?"

"Perhaps," I said with a sneaky smirk. "But only on one condition."

His head tilted, waiting for me to name my demand.

"You get in with me."

"I can think of no place I'd rather be," Liam said.

It didn't take long for us to strip each other of our clothes. Though it was by far not the first time he had seen me bare, it still left me with bashful delight to feel his eyes on me—until my own watchful gaze made its way like a serpent down his naked flesh. My nostrils flared with my rising libido as I allowed him to help me into the tub.

By the time I began lowering myself into the perfect-temperature water, he was waiting for me. He held his hand out in a cradled position, crafting my body so that it molded back into his. Once his arms snaked around my ribs, I closed my eyes and leaned my head back onto his shoulder.

Within minutes of being in Liam's arms, the shitty day had disappeared.

"Do you want to tell me about your day?" Liam asked while his hand trailed up and down my arm.

"No…" He kissed my temple softly, remaining silent. "Yes."

He chuckled at my waver as he pressed his face into the back of my hair.

"No fair," I said.

"What?" Liam asked innocently.

"When you have me like this, I feel like I could reveal state secrets."

I wiggled my neck as if trying to encourage him to get as close to me as possible. He obliged by kissing my shoulder and wrapping his arms around my stomach. He said nothing more, waiting for me to either continue or abandon the subject.

"What does this feel like for you?"

I rippled the water by bringing my hand above the surface.

"You don't have to change the subject if you don't want to talk about him."

I smiled, amazed at how he had known about Michael without any words. He didn't need to read my mind to be in tune with me.

"You know what? I don't want to talk about Michael." I rubbed my hand reassuringly against Liam's. "But not because I don't want you to know about how shitty it makes me feel."

I waited, feeling his nod as he aligned his temple with mine, urging me to continue without fear of judgment.

"It's just that being like this with you makes me realize something."

"What's that?" Liam said.

"I'm tired of carrying around this guilt that comes from loving you."

It was funny how I said I didn't want to talk about it and yet here I was, venting.

"I shouldn't have to feel guilty for being in love with you. And that doesn't mean I don't empathize with him for not having his feelings for me reciprocated. Of course I do…and I hate that I'm the one who hurt him."

I paused, unable to finish the thought. It was as if Liam could feel my blood boil with anger as my body tensed within his arms. His fingers once again soothed me by trailing up my arm.

"I can only imagine how much more complicated things would be if he still carried these fake memories too."

My voice was low, as if my energy to the thoughts behind them had drained me.

"Some days he makes me feel as if there were teams and I chose the wrong one. Except he doesn't realize that there was never anyone to choose between. You are and will always be the one I love."

"I know it's frustrating but just give him some more time. He's a good guy and from what I've come to know, he won't be able to resist wanting to keep you in his life. No matter what type of relationship that may be."

"Yeah?"

"I'm certain no one would be able to resist the chance to have you in their life."

I smirked, as if he had set off a notification alert in my brain that was unable to stop myself itself from tallying the reasons why I loved him. I closed my eyes for a moment, hearing the words within my mind.

Reason 146.

CHAPTER 6

NORMAL

A week later, when Erika extended an invitation onto her uncle's boat, it felt like the perfect timing for a welcome distraction—a night to help me forget about my strained friendship with Michael and the unnerving wait for a vengeful immortal.

But mostly it was an overdue moment to be normal for a night. To indulge in the life moments of a high school senior, which were usually filled with the excitement of prom, the worry of college admissions, and the sadness of saying goodbye to the people you grew up with.

"If you get bored, I'm sure Sean will be happy to tell you all the things I say about you."

I bit my bottom lip while looking over at Liam teasingly as he pulled into the closest spot near the docks.

"I'm counting on it."

I could hear the amusement in his voice as I turned my head to see Becca and Pamela standing near a boat tied to the far east end dock.

"I'll call you when everything is wrapping up."

He leaned over the console to find my waiting lips and held them against his own with a kiss that was longer than anticipated. For a minute I debated whether to follow my intoxicated state, which beckoned me to stay in the car with him—at least until my eyes found the sinister smirk that gave away his mission.

I pulled back, opening my mouth to protest, only to be met by a light-hearted surrender that his upward palms demonstrated.

"I'll wait for your call," Liam said while sitting back against his seat.

I shook my head, unable to hold off my smile as I stepped out of the car. The cold breeze was occupied by the strong, dry decay of fish. It was an acquired smell, to be honest.

Making my way down the dock, I couldn't help but turn back to study the sunset as if it were a friend whispering for my attention. Watching the sky helplessly surrender to the darkness was always my favorite part of the day.

"I didn't realize you were so into sunsets."

I turned and continued the short walk toward my friends.

"Who isn't?" I said.

Becca shrugged as she stepped nervously onto the deck, using her arms to balance herself even though the boat remained still. It was no secret that she had never learned to swim, which made activities involving water her least favorite choices. Pamela, on the other hand, was the opposite, stepping onto the boat with a swimmer's confidence that radiated down to her wiggling fingers.

"I've always liked the moon more myself," Becca said.

My eyebrows rose as I placed my other leg onto the boat, knowing exactly where the conversation was heading.

"Honestly, she reads one series about werewolves and—"

"Don't pretend you weren't mildly obsessed with vampires for a month after *Twilight* came out."

"Yes, but I didn't start loving the sunlight because of it."

"Well, technically you wouldn't worship the sun if you were a vampire, would you?"

I remained silent, listening to the argument with an odd enjoyment.

"Dude, I'd so rather be a werewolf than a vampire," Becca said.

"Oh my god, why?" Pamela asked incredulously. "They have to break their bones every time they transform."

"You'd rather burn in the sunlight?"

"Nah, I'd just get a daylight ring," Pamela said as if it were the most obvious solution.

"Not everyone can get one of those. You'd have to know a witch, dummy."

"Emma, any chance you come from a long line of witches?" Pamela asked in a teasing manner.

It was amazing how right Liam was about immortals. We had no idea of their existence because they were perfectly hidden within the imagination of our human minds.

If only my friends knew that the fictional vampires they joked about were ones they would never want to meet. Even I still felt an icy chill run down my spine as I remembered Liam's warning about those who chose to be vampiric immortals.

But tonight was about being normal. For once, I lowered my guard of constant fear and let out the teenage girl who was ready to enjoy the night with my friends.

"Perhaps…" I paused while clicking my tongue in mock seriousness. "But I don't make daylight rings for just anyone. You'll have to earn it."

Pamela held onto the railing as her neck turned slightly enough for me to see her scrunched lips shifting from side to side with the small nod of her head.

"What about buying you pizza for life?"

Becca ducked beneath the lower deck as she laughed. "That's the worst deal ever."

"What?" Pamela raised her arms in protest. "Even witches love free pizza."

"Whose getting free pizza?"

My torso bent slightly so that I could duck below deck. Once I was able to stand at my full height again, my eyes lifted to the unexpected space. The interior wood panels had been painted blue, which stood out against the white cushioned seats that were long enough for four people to lay down if they wanted.

"Oh, Pamela here is offering free pizza to get herself a daylight ring."

"That would depend on the witch," Erika said, jumping in perfectly as if playing a game of double-dutch.

"In this case, it's Emma."

Pamela's thumb pointed back at me as she sat on the middle cushion next to Becca.

"Books." I turned to my left to see Lauren looking up at me with a wink. "I'd offer to buy you a new book every day to read."

"Deal," I said with a smirk before stepping forward and playfully shaking Lauren's extended hand.

"Looks like you lost that ring," Becca teased

"Why don't you offer the promise of never hitting on Liam?"

Finally, my eyes looked over to the far right corner that Becca had been unintentionally blocking with her body. Heather looked up at me with pink cheeks and curled lips of boredom.

"That's worse than the pizza offer," Becca mumbled.

"Oh…I didn't know you were coming tonight," I said.

"Well, I heard Erika talking in the hallway to Lauren about a girls' night and I thought it sounded like fun." She tilted her head, her voice rising with a high, condescending tone. "Why, did you not want me here?"

I shook my head, quick to protest. "No, I think we're all happy to have you." *As long as you aren't a bitch.* "It's been a while since we've all been together anyway."

The irony was that nothing could feel more *high school* than being around Heather. The thought forced me to turn around swiftly so that she wouldn't see the smirk plastered on my face.

As I made my way over to sit next to Lauren, I could see she was better at keeping her composure. If I hadn't seen the little twitch from her nose I would never have known that she was resisting a laugh.

I teasingly bumped her shoulder as I sat down and took in the perfect volume of the music. Erika had set it so that we could hear the lyrics but it wasn't loud enough to force us to yell over it to have a conversation.

"Emma, do you want something to drink?" Erika said as she held open the top of a red cooler with her right hand, her face already positioned forward.

"Oh, um, do you have any Sprite?"

Erika smiled before reaching in to retrieve a green bottle.

"Here," she said, handing me the Sprite before making her way up the steps to pull the hatch door shut. We were left to the light of the small windows that were slowly darkening as the sun dropped below the horizon.

Before sitting, Erika flipped a switch near the bow, turning on several small lights throughout the inside of the cabin.

"You know who would make a great vampire? Liam."

My head snapped around at Pamela's words. I watched the way she held up her hand and looked around for validation.

"I think it takes more than pretty eyes to be supernatural," I said.

"That's true." Pamela paused, nodding her head as if I'd made a valid point. "But tell me they don't have that *Underworld* glow sometimes. Am I right?"

"Wait," Erika said with her finger raised. "Don't all the vampires in those movies have bright *blue* eyes?"

"Oh yeah," Pamela said with lips protruding in disappointment.

I sat quietly listening, observing, but ultimately remaining uninvolved with any contribution.

"The Alexander twins." Becca clapped as if she had just guessed the topic in a game of charades.

"Yesss," Pamela said, nudging Becca. "Good one, Becks."

Several heads nodded in agreement while I simply rolled my eyes.

"Regardless, those are some good genes," Becca said.

"You and Liam would probably have kids who ended up having the same stunning green eyes," Pamela added.

As I shrugged at the comment, my hand instinctively touched my silver bracelet. My cheeks reddened as I became the target of everyone's gaze, helpless against the awkwardness seeping into the atmosphere.

"So…how is Sean doing? Does he like UNC?"

"He's happy there," I said, grinning with a nod of appreciation toward Lauren's welcomed interruption.

"I can see why." She paused with a knowing smile at what she had done. "I visited over Christmas break and loved it."

"Did you send off your application yet?"

Lauren's mouth straightened but her lips nervously moved against one another. "Yeah, but I also applied to Duke just to get my dad off my case."

"I get that," I said rolling my eyes at the memories that flooded back. "My dad had been trying to influence Sean and me from the moment he was able to convince my mom to dress us in Duke onesies. So, I'm sure if he were here, he'd be pestering me about applying there too."

Though she tried to hide it, I could see the small pity within Lauren's eyes.

"Where did you apply?" she asked, as if hoping the soft turn would gear us away from the uncomfortable reality.

"Well, as of now...nowhere," I said with a shrug. "But I'm sure UNC and Duke will be on my list in the next few weeks."

I grinned easily with the lie, unsure if that made me feel proud or uneasy. But then again, even if my primary goal over the next few months wasn't to stay alive, the college decision was a unique one.

Perhaps it was why my lie held some truth when I told my friend about applying to two North Carolina schools—two colleges that I knew were in the Alexanders' territory.

Lauren nodded and turned her attention back to the group, just as Becca turned her gaze on me. *Oh no.*

"Sorry, I have to ask," Becca said, leaning forward with a small grin that told me she wasn't *genuinely* sorry but instead was looking for a gossip thrill. "What happened with you and Michael?"

"What do you mean?"

My body stiffened and my brow rose as my eyes shifted over to see the identical and yet not unexpected curiosity that Pamela carried.

"Well, you two seemed to have gotten *close* after Liam left."

"Hmm," I said with a reluctant nod.

"And now Liam's back and you don't seem as *close*..."

Becca drifted off, gesturing with her left hand in a forward circular motion.

"I think you just answered your own question," I said.

"Well, we can all see some major awkwardness so...did anything *actually* happen with Michael or is he just jealous?"

Pamela jumped in like a teammate who had just been slapped into the wrestling ring by her partner.

Screw it.

"No, nothing ever happened but things are *awkward*..." I paused, looking at Pamela directly. "Because he told me that he was in love with me."

"Whoa," the girls said in unison.

"Unrequited love is the worst," Becca added.

"How would you know?" Pamela asked, looking back over and raising her finger in the air as if anticipating Becca's next sentence. "I swear, if you mention something about werewolves..."

"I wasn't," Becca said but her sudden silence told the rest of us that this was exactly what she was going to say.

"I feel horrible because he's always been there for me. Especially when my dad died." My eyes bounced to the ground, unwilling to focus on the expected pity of my words. Seeing Lauren's pity earlier, even if briefly, was enough. "But I can't apologize for being in love with someone else."

"We get it," Lauren said.

"Thanks," I said.

I was hopeful the conversation spotlight would shift to someone else. Thankfully, as if Erika had heard my silent plea, the next victim was chosen.

"Speaking of apologizing, Becca…"

Hours later, we all sat chuckling as Pamela mocked her boyfriend, Kyle Bellmen. The smile I held was finally genuine, as I'd been granted my wish: to revel in the normality of my old life without the tense spotlight of talking about my new one.

The laughter in the cabin was at its loudest of the night. Even Heather was joining in with us. Then a thud drew our attention to the starboard side of the boat.

"What was that?" Heather asked.

Without a need for a command, Erika turned down the music. She stood silent, listening as she stared at the ground. After a few seconds of silence, she looked back at the group with a shrug.

"Something probably fell that wasn't secure on deck. I'll check it out to be sure."

She jogged up the steps and creaked open the door hatch to make her way onto the deck. We all sat silent, waiting for news of what she would discover.

"Oh my god," Erika whined out.

56

I was out of my seat and up the steps before any of the others had moved. When I reached the doorway I stepped onto the deck only to be met with a darkness that forced me to blink excessively to adjust to the sight.

But my stomach tensed, as I knew that it was taking too long to adjust to the dark when we were so close to the docks. I turned to use the lampposts from the boardwalk as a guide only to realize there were none. My eyes had finally begun to adjust enough to stiffen at the sight.

There were no lampposts because we weren't near the docks. There was no light except for the cabin lights from below deck. And just as the other girls began to shout out, "What the hell," and "Oh my god," I felt my own unease. We were stranded in the middle of the Pamlico River.

I looked to Erika, who seemed to be pleading with me for an explanation—one that I didn't have.

"I swear the boat was securely tied up to the dock. And even then, it would be impossible without the engine on, right?"

She was scratching her head while looking in all directions, clearly panicking, as most would. But glancing beyond her toward the bow, my eyes caught sight of the problem. *Shit.*

So much for being normal.

CHAPTER 7

FIRST WAVE

I should have known better. It was one thing to appear as if life continued on but another to openly expose my friends to danger because I was lost in a craving for normality. Normal was a stranger to me and I should have known I could no longer try to befriend it. I should have known my selfish decision would have consequences.

My eyes shifted, as if I had my own radar for seeing the threat before my friends. But it wasn't long before the immortal stepped forward with a slow and painfully dramatic walk until he exposed himself with a controlled stomp on the deck. I knew instantly it was the same motion he had made to summon us all up here. Only this time the mere vibration commanded the two floodlights above our heads to come to life.

Becca shrieked but my gaze remained at the immortal's feet, watching as he crept forward, walking with a playful tightrope precision. His other leg lifted and dropped swiftly with the same vibration, forcing on the bright horizontal bulbs on each side of the boat.

My chin followed my stare upward, taking in the black combat boots that merged with his dark-colored wardrobe of outdated grunge. His raven hair curled slightly but stopped above his ears. It all stood out in contrast to the pale illumination of his alabaster face and the brightness of his golden topaz eyes.

His body drew close and he turned his neck slightly to each of us with a focused gaze that felt like a twisted game of musical chairs. As soon as his eyes met mine, he stopped moving and his neck pulled back in a grin.

"Who are you?" Erika asked.

As the others moved inward toward me, Erika confidently stepped forward. I tensed at her bravery and instinctively lifted my arm to pull at her shirt. I felt relief when she dropped her gaze back toward the ground. But it was short-lived, as if her bravery had been dunked underwater and then suddenly resurfaced.

"This is my uncle's boat and…you…you're trespassing."

It didn't go unnoticed that her voice trembled throughout her intended threat. The immortal held a raised brow and exhaled with a small chuckle that told me he was amused. It was like a human letting an ant crawl on their hand seconds before crushing it to death with their fingers.

"I apologize."

The immortal spoke with an unexpected calm, velvet tone that almost hypnotized you into believing he was there to help. It was the worst kind of evil—the kind that lured you into a safe cocoon of deception.

He stepped closer, his full gaze upon me in odd excitement, as if we had known each other for years and finally had the opportunity to reunite.

"Hello, Emma."

My eyes locked on his, my back straightening in alert to the danger I was helpless to avoid. The only question I had left was what their orders were. I wasn't stupid enough to think that Thomas would make things so simple.

"You know him?"

Pamela spoke with a tone like that of an undecided cat walking on a fence. It started with blame but then that emotion was pulled back, replaced with a small sense of hope that was convinced I could be the one to make him leave.

"No," I said with a low and yet clear voice that made it obvious I had no way of pulling the reins on this animal.

"She doesn't know me but I certainly know *her*."

I knew he was merely narrating the point in the sadistic hope of terrorizing my friends but his gaze lingered on me with a creepy admiration.

"Would you mind leaving, then?"

I turned toward Lauren, whose sweet and firm voice had given the polite order. As soon as his eyes shifted, I knew I had to draw him back, even if that resulted in the stare I wished to escape seconds ago.

"Don't hurt them," I demanded.

His neck turned back toward me but it took a few seconds for his narrowed predator gaze to lift from Lauren. I was certain that if I hadn't spoken up he would have choked Lauren to death, if not done something worse.

"I…" I stumbled with my words, the fear radiating off my skin. "I know you're here for me so just get on with it, but leave them alone."

His shoulders rose with a pretentious breath that I knew his immortal body didn't need. His eyes looked off in contemplation while his lips held a straight line.

"Okay," he said, shifting his gaze back to me with an agreeable nod. "I won't touch your friends."

I exhaled in victorious relief before realizing that there was a small tremor in my hand. But as I looked down, I found that I wasn't the one causing the movement. Erika had grasped my hand with her own and was unable to control her involuntary shake. I lifted my chin to focus on her short breaths and terrified gaze above our heads.

Damn it.

My eyes glanced forward, waiting like a countdown until, seconds later, the new member of the party appeared in front of us. I didn't need to look to know she had probably flipped in the air with a reflexive stealth that was performed for our benefit.

"I can't say the same for Fiona."

My shoulders slumped as I noticeably gulped. Fiona wore a pair of skin-tight leather pants that she had tucked inside knee-length boots. Her wavy black hair stopped at the center of her neck and the striking, glowing blue orb of her eyes caused me to think back to the lighthearted teasing my friends had engaged in earlier about *Underworld.*

It was then that Fiona's expression became somewhat giddy, as if she'd been given a new toy to play with. She stepped closer to our huddled group, eyeing us like a stealth panther as her lips curved in satisfaction over what I assumed was the surfaced fear we all carried.

Unfortunately, I knew the predator had finally laid eyes on its inevitable target. *Erika.* And even though she had controlled her shaking, Erika had paled at the unwanted attention. Her body stiffened as the immortal licked her lips and extended her neck to inhale near my friend's jawline. Erika remained impressively still, even as the immortal pulled back and looked at her companion with a pleading smile.

"Please say we have time for me to have a taste?"

The small gasp behind me was proof that the English accent with which the immortal spoke made her "Kate Beckinsale doppelgänger" appearance impossible to ignore.

Her partner in crime side-eyed her, making a sound as if he wasn't sure it was a good idea. I watched the subtle glance toward the silver watch occupying his wrist and knew his hesitance wasn't because he found Fiona's behavior morally wrong. It was because they were limited on time.

"Come on, Ben. You know you owe me for interrupting my last...craving."

It was a sardonic, playful moment between the two immortals, Fiona puckering her lips like a little girl begging to get her way. Her partner was simply amused by her antics.

"Fair enough," Ben said with a go-ahead motion of his hand. "But we have time for you to pick only *one*."

My eyes widened and Liam's words echoed in my mind. *Some have acquired the taste. Great,* I thought as, suddenly, our *Underworld* comparison was complete for the night.

I shook my head, unwilling to let her kill one of my friends that way—at least not before putting up some resistance. My instinct readied my body to lunge at the immortal, even if it were a mere distraction, something that sped up the clock and forced them to move ahead with their orders involving me. It felt like an impulse rather than a rational decision but it was too late to turn back.

"Actually, wait..." Fiona stepped forward, her hand flat against my chest, already knowing my plan seconds before I implemented it. She looked back at Ben, the two of them holding an identical victorious grin.

"You know, it's funny that I count five bodies and yet..." She paused, turning back to her partner's wink as if she were a professor lecturing her students.

"I can *hear* six heartbeats."

Fiona turned her gaze back in our direction but it was as if she wasn't looking at us, but behind us.

"It will be so much worse for you if you make me come down there," Fiona said.

We all turned in unison toward the sound on the steps. I shook my head, shocked at how the stress and fear had led us all to forget that Heather had remained below deck while the rest of us had run up at Erika's original distress.

"Don't much have a craving for cowards I'm afraid, blondie," Fiona said, eyeing Heather with a curled lip of disgust. "Although that doesn't mean I couldn't—"

"Fi," Ben said with a warning tone, reminding her that the timing wouldn't allow her to play with her food much longer.

My mind told my feet to move with that same instinct again but suddenly, within my blink, I found I had control over nothing *except* for my blinks. What was worse was being unaware of the movement and suddenly taking in my new position, which was held firmly in place by Ben. I wasn't standing with my friends anymore but looking *toward* them, taking in the different levels of fear and confusion each of them carried.

"No time for heroics," Ben said while lowering his nose to my hair and whispering out the words in an intimate fashion.

"Let go of her," Erika said.

I wanted to shake my head, tell her that while I was grateful, the thing I needed was her silence. Not to draw attention to herself. I wanted to say this but the sudden immortal grasp of my head prevented me from doing anything. And it seemed that was the point, so that I would be forced to watch the outcome like some horrific play. That was when I knew.

"You're not here to kill me, are you?"

"Well, you are a clever one, aren't you?" he said with a whisper in my ear. I closed my eyes, knowing it was the only escape from the unwanted embrace. Or so I thought. "Do I have to open those eyes of yours too?"

The thought of his deadly fingers anywhere near my face forced me to lift my eyelids instantly. Just as Ben rested his temple against mine, I could see Becca and Pamela trying to move quietly back toward the stern while Fiona held her focus on Erika. She glanced back at me, flicking her brow as if to taunt me.

"She looks delicious," Fiona said while delicately sweeping Erika's long, dark hair off the left side of her neck.

The other four girls had huddled into a group of protection, carrying a mixture of fear and confusion as their gazes bounced from me to Erika.

"Is this real?" Becca said with a trembling voice that caught Fiona's attention.

"Would you like to feel just how real it is?"

Becca whimpered, stepping as close to Pamela as their bodies would physically allow.

There was no doubt I held my own fear, one that I had probably held since the day Katherine died. But outside of that expected fear was a layered frustration that had boiled over in anger. "They have nothing to do with the Alexanders or Thomas."

Fiona merely looked at Ben with a Cheshire cat smile, enjoying the inside joke between them.

"Your time will come, Emma," Fiona said.

"But not tonight?"

The immortals chuckled in unison, aware that their silence to the question was more irritating than the intimidation of fear. I was left helpless, closing my eyes for the briefest moment while reluctantly commending them on how well executed it all was. Their still-immortal precision was crucial to a plan that would not alert me to any danger.

They knew going in that they needed me blind as they released and led the boat down the exposed body of water. The GPS connection I held with Sean would be delayed. And that delay meant there was a high chance that, once I was found, one—if not all—of my friends would be dead.

I fought off the wetness that glistened at my eyes, lucky that a distraction appeared to help with the useless need to cry. I took in Heather's noticeable shifting glances, certain her mind was in the process of scoping out the best angle for abandoning the boat and saving herself. At least that was until I watched the unexpected way she charged forward, like a battle warrior, toward Fiona.

Before I could scream, "Heather, don't," her body was already twisting into the air with a backward momentum. Then it collided with the port side of the boat. I winced at her unconscious body, quickly focusing on the imprint of blood left inside the small indent of metal.

Fiona's mouth slowly lifted like an opening night curtain and she smiled in cruel delight as she glanced at me. Her lips parted, exposing her white teeth for a few seconds before she sank them viciously into Erika's exposed neck. My friend released a piercing scream that was fueled by terror and a pain that I imagined came from the razor sharpness of Fiona's teeth penetrating her skin.

"No!"

My angered plea went unheard as the sound coming from Erika's throat began to weaken into a whimper. I felt a small vibration at my feet as Becca fainted. Lauren and Pamela froze, desperately wanting to check on her but terrified to move an inch without permission. Lauren was more willing, it seemed, with her foot suddenly angled toward the still unconscious Heather.

Fiona's head tilted back off Erika's neck with a look of pure orgasmic joy. Her mouth hung open, letting her body absorb the satisfying high before her tongue greedily licked the leftover blood off her lips. She held Erika close, with her arm crossed over her chest, as if claiming her even in her drug-infused state.

"Fiona," Ben said with a warning tone to make his vampiric immortal partner snap back with a nod of understanding.

While I hoped his urgency meant the sand was running out for them, I simultaneously feared for those last moments. It was similar to cornering a snake that we knew had a lethal bite when provoked.

"Until next time, Emma," Ben whispered with the same uneasy velvet tone.

There wasn't time to even grimace before my body was thrown over the boat and into the cold water. My feet had barely kicked out with an effort to raise my head above the surface when I heard a series of screams and other splashes hitting the frigid water.

The boat made a load crunching roar, pieces flying off into the water around us. I blinked, seeing the way it took in water, knowing it was inevitably starting its descent below the surface.

But I knew the bigger problem was the temperature of the water. My mind was already beginning to lose focus. I kept moving my arms and legs in large circles, my body desperate to give up as the sound of another engine echoed like laughter fading into the distance.

I attempted to turn my neck and quickly caught sight of a dark, limp figure that was unnaturally floating near me. It was Erika. I pushed my arms with heavy breaths, trying to ignore the sting of my hands and the energy it was taking to move mere inches in the cold water. By some helpful twist of luck, I reached a floating piece of wreckage near her right side, then swung both of her arms over the wood so that her head was no longer face down. Once I knew she was secure, I reached over to grasp onto the wreckage and prevent myself from losing any more energy—in my arms at least.

"I can't swim!"

From somewhere on my left, I heard Becca. I didn't need to see her face to comprehend the seeping panic in her voice. While the rest of us were dealing with the threat of hypothermia, she had the added nightmare of possibly drowning.

"Quit kicking like that. You're making it worse," I heard Pamela shout with irritation. My head turned to understand the frustration that came from the energy it was taking for her to kick herself closer to Becca while dragging two round life preservers she must have found from the boat.

"I'm sorry."

Becca's voice had balanced out from her previous shouting.

"I...know," Pamela grunted as she pushed one of the preservers within Becca's grasp before swinging her arms inside the other.

"Lauren," I shouted, unsure where the energy had erupted from.

"Over here," Lauren hollered. I squinted across the small distance until I was able to see her hand wave in the darkness. "I found Heather."

"Is she okay?"

"I don't know...I found a life ring...from the boat...to put on...her" I was grateful that Erika's uncle had stocked the boat with more than one life preserver. "I think her head...is banged up...pretty bad...where's Erika?"

Lauren's voice remained came but it didn't go unnoticed that she needed many breaks between her speech.

"I have her," I confirmed but by either fear or occupation with Heather, Lauren remained silent upon my answer.

That silence was interrupted when the bow of the boat shot a gush of water into the air. It rained down like melted ice as the powerful suction helped the water claim its victim. Carefully, I reached out to move Erika's head so that I could inspect the wound on her neck with my stiff hand. My throat instantly tightened when I saw the vicious indention that was a perfect mold of Fiona's immortal teeth.

I shivered at the realization of how intense and powerful a bite would have to be with teeth that resembled our own human shape. I wasn't sure if I was more disgusted or terrified at such an act.

"I'm so cold," Becca said.

It was low and faint, almost a whisper.

"I know," I said, closing my eyes as if that would help give me strength. "Just hang on a little longer."

"No one knows we're out here."

Pamela seemed to voice what I was certain the others all feared. And for that, I hoped the rescue party was close. *Please hurry.*

"Are we going to die?"

Neither Pamela nor I answered, desperate to stay away from the unknown of the question. To be honest, it was the last thing I wanted to think about with Erika's limp body so close to me. Instead, I let my mind drift to Liam—his warm body, his soft lips, his heavenly scent around me.

"Do you hear that?"

At this point, I couldn't be certain who had said the words but I was positive I could hear the sound of a motor. My mind alerted my senses, my eyes searching in the distance.

"It's a boat," Lauren said.

"It's two," Pamela's voice rang with both triumph and fear.

"What if they came back?" Becca stammered.

Driven by instinct, I began to shout, "Liam!"

"What are you doing?"

Pamela's voice was strained and yet irritated by my behavior as the engines drew closer.

"Emma!"

Liam shouted back as if we were playing a game of Marco Polo. I sighed, feeling a small grin of relief to hear the sound of Liam's angelic and worried tone.

The oncoming noise of the engines was met with a spotlight shining down on the water's surface, bouncing between us. Pamela instinctively waved her free arm as if signaling the rescue. Suddenly, another light shined closer, forcing me to squint up at the brightness as the engines went quiet.

"Emma," Liam said with a controlled edge, already claiming my body as he reached into the water, unaffected in the slightest by the cold.

"Take her," I pleaded but it seemed as though Liam refused to let me out of his reach. Grace was already swooping in and delicately grabbed Erika's limp body.

Unfortunately, as Liam pulled me out of the water's reach, it was like the breaking of a dam. The cold breeze stung my weakened body, which was already shaking and made worse by the damp frozen clothes hanging off me.

Immediately, I was engulfed by a thick blanket and the added warmth of Liam's body as he sat, pulling me between his legs and holding both the blanket and me with a tight possession. If I thought it was hard to focus before, it was worse now as the shock of my body began to seep in like an intruder. It was only because my body was already facing straight that I could see

Grace and Mary on each side of Erika, whom they had laid flat on a pair of thick blankets.

"Ssssshe wwasss bbbitttten."

My teeth chattered through the words, causing Liam to place his temple against mine as the boat's engine came back to life.

"Yes, her body has almost been drained completely," Mary said with her hand on the side of Erika's neck as she spoke with the distracted tone you would expect from a doctor during surgery.

"Is ssshe dddead?"

I tried to convince my exhausted mind that it was better to know but I was terrified to hear the answer.

"I've healed the wound but she needs blood urgently."

The numbness loudly beckoned for me to stop fighting. As if sensing my movement, Liam moved his head just in time for me to lay my head back against his collarbone. I felt a small, tender kiss on my scalp just as my eyes closed on command and my mind drifted into an easy sleep.

CHAPTER 8

SCARRED

It always intrigued me how suddenly the human mind could go from deep sleep to conscious thought. One moment I was drowning in a black void and then, all at once, I was thinking about how grateful I was to be dry and warm.

My fingers twitched against the fleece blanket that I could feel on my legs and resting above my torso. The heavy dampness of my hair was suddenly gone, from root to end, no longer tainted by the tang of saltwater.

The fresh lavender I inhaled beckoned me to finally open my eyes with a satisfied grin. It was a scent that Liam had added for me in his room after I had mentioned only once that it was my favorite.

"Emma."

Liam's calm, soft voice pulled my focus down to him as he sat on the bed near my hip. He leaned down, gently moving the back of his hand to trace my face. It was as if he were trying to leave an imprint for his memory later. I turned my head slightly and looked up into his brightened emerald gaze.

"Hi," I said.

I placed my hand over his, which was resting on my jawline.

"How are you feeling?" Liam asked.

"Sore," I admitted, quite aware that he would have already seen me wince seconds earlier as I attempted to move my legs.

I had to admit, there was a bit of déjà vu in waking up in Liam's bed again after another traumatic event. Except unlike with Henry's attack, there was one difference. It wasn't an attack on just me.

"Where are my friends?"

I couldn't bear to frame the question another way and yet I waited with trepidation for Liam to rip off the band-aid.

"Sean and Lillian took the other four home a few hours ago." My breath hitched, catching quickly when he said "four." "Heather had a mere concussion and a broken wrist but Mary was able to easily mend that. Luckily, the other three didn't suffer any major injuries."

I knew by that he meant they had most likely suffered effects of hypothermia, like I had, but it wasn't uncommon for Liam to avoid the details. Especially because I knew Mary wouldn't allow them to leave if they weren't well enough.

"What about…"

At my hesitance, he rubbed my cheek with his thumb, attempting to relax my suddenly tense muscles.

"She's alive."

I closed my eyes and released a grateful sigh, despite the weight that lingered in my stomach from guilt. I felt Liam's soft lips against my forehead, pulling me out of my distracted thoughts.

My neck straightened and I gazed into the comfort of his bright emerald eyes. Liam sat looking back at me with an adoring grin that reminded me I wasn't the only one grateful for the outcome of last night.

"Where is she?"

"She's recovering in the hospital downstairs."

I could feel my arched brow of confusion even before I spoke the words.

"You know, I've toured this mansion several times and I've never seen a hospital."

He tried to resist another grin but it was hard to tell if he was unsuccessful or just happy about my distraction.

"Mary's been a little busy lately."

"Hmm…" I looked around the room as my mind contemplated the interactions I had shared with Mary the past month. She had definitely made herself distant lately, much like when Liam and I had first started dating.

"I guess you're right."

Liam raised his hand to place a few fallen strands of hair behind my ear.

"We've all dealt with Jane's proposal differently. While some are more vocal..." Liam paused. We both knew who he was talking about without his needing to say it aloud. "Mary's method was taking on the project of creating a surgical space in case we need it for you."

"She built a hospital room...just for *me*?"

"Yes," Liam confirmed.

Though I was beyond touched by Mary's affection, it was easier to shift the focus away from me.

"How long does Erika have to stay?"

For the first time, I saw avoidance in Liam's gaze, but I knew he would never lie to me.

"Mary has cleared her medically but Patrick hasn't modified her memory as of yet."

My throat dried instantly and I felt the pinch from underneath my chest. If someone looked close enough, they would see the tender scars tattooed around the pumping muscle. Perhaps even William could see them with his gift.

"Was he intentionally waiting for me to see her first?"

As soon as Liam nodded, I attempted to move my legs, immediately feeling the soreness of my body again.

Liam, unable to bear the slight grimace, picked me up and cradled my body to his own. It was only a few seconds before he was gently placing my feet to the ground in front of an open doorway on the first floor of the mansion.

My neck pulled back as my eyes widened at the sight of the powder blue walls of the large room. Each side was split as if designed to be its own department. On one side was extensive testing machinery, while on the other stood a small functional operating area. In the corner, next to a white freezer, was a blue vertical blood bank fridge, full of blood bags.

"Emma?"

I heard Erika's voice from the far left of the room, where a small hospital bed was positioned near a set of machines. I shook my head out of my entranced state before turning to see her relief as she sat up from the bed.

I walked over to her, quickly sitting on a stool near her left hip. I glanced over at the high-tech monitor displaying her vitals, uncertain why I was suddenly at a loss for words.

"Well, your heart rate looks good," I joked.

"Yeah," she said with a smile before her eyes pleaded for me to bend closer. "Do you remember what happened?"

"Yes."

Despite her cautious tone, I spoke at a normal volume. I could tell by her slightly stiffened body and widened gaze that she was bothered by my lack of a whisper.

"Do they know…I mean, have you told them exactly what happened? That I was…" It was as if Erika didn't know how to finish her thoughts, let alone questions. I understood, more than anyone, that feeling of discovering something beyond your belief for the first time: the confusion, the excitement, the fear.

I sat back slightly, my eyes shifting over to Mary and Liam as they stood with their backs to us in the far corner of the room.

"Yes, they know."

It felt odd that for the longest time I had slightly craved to share the secret of being a human within the immortal world, while now I wasn't willing to unlock that vault to anyone. I had not intended to be vague with my words but in the last seconds I became cautious, much like the immortals would be with humans.

Of course, I could still have divulged everything if only to clear my conscience because I knew that in mere minutes, her memory would be wiped anyhow. But the familiar violation distanced me enough to refrain.

I fought off nausea as I stood, patting her hand.

"Well, I'm still feeling a bit tired," I said while holding my smile without suspicion. "And I know you need some rest so..."

She nodded in understanding, as I was already walking toward the doorway. My eyes closed briefly with a small sigh. I was grateful to find a pair of bright concerned emerald eyes staring back at me as soon as they opened.

"Did you ever catch up with them?"

His smile vanished with anger but he remained silent, merely shaking his head. I didn't need the verbal confirmation to know that the Alexanders had focused on my friends and me instead of Thomas's first launch team.

"Oh, no!"

Erika's raised terror alerted me, causing Liam to pull his arm protectively around the front of my body.

"My uncle's boat. It's..."

I released the breath I had been holding and relaxed my forehead against Liam's arm.

"I can help with that."

All eyes, including my own, turned to see Patrick coming into the room with a bedside-mannered smile. As he caught sight of me, his gaze lingered, as if he was experiencing his own sense of relief at the sight of me awake.

Patrick shifted his gaze to Mary, who nodded so subtly I would have missed it had I not been looking in their direction. My focus on them had even missed Grace's agile steps in the doorway.

"Good to see you awake, Emma," Grace said, lightly touching my forearm before making her way over to my friend.

Before Erika's eyes could reveal the familiarity of Grace from memory, my immortal sister-in-law had sent the girl off into a deep sleep at the mere touch of her shoulder.

"Come on," Liam said, sliding his hand into mine.

"Wait," I said, placing my other hand against Liam's chest. My eyes looked up to his with a new plea. "I want to watch."

"Emma." Liam's voice held a warning hesitancy. It seemed he couldn't find the right words but I knew he meant, "I don't think you want to see this."

I shook my head, uncertain of it myself. "I don't *want* to see but I *need* to."

"It's her choice," Patrick said.

His tone made it clear that I wasn't the only one affected by the choice of what they had done to my own memory. Liam used the back of his index finger to outline my cheekbone before he finally stepped back, though he was not willing to let go of my hand.

Without further hesitation, Patrick leaned over to wrap his hand around Erika's head as if he were sizing her for a royal crown. His thumbs rested on the middle of her forehead and he looked down at her face before closing his eyes in concentration.

My breathing was heavy and I squeezed Liam's hand with a harsh grip. His immortal strength didn't feel discomfort but he gently squeezed back with reassurance as if to say, *I'm here.*

After what felt like minutes of anguish but was probably only seconds, Patrick lifted his hands. His bright eyes opened and shifted over to mine. My throat burned and my breathing shortened. I attempted to push down the fear I remembered in that moment when my own memory was taken, but it merely floated on the surface.

"What will she remember?"

"Just as they all do, that you all went to eat and then headed home for the night."

"And her uncle's boat?"

"She remembers that he sold it a year ago, as will her uncle."

"Oh," I said, listening to him tell me about her new memory as if he were telling me his class schedule for the semester. It was so simple, without the slightest need for thought. That was what made it so terrifying.

Suddenly, I dropped Liam's hand and turned to walk out of the room, needing as much distance from that room as possible.

I continued walking without direction, as if trying to outrun my mind.

Before I realized that I was walking toward the front door, it had opened on its own—thanks to Liam—allowing me to walk through and head down the porch steps. All the memories, both real and fake, were swirling up to the surface without my control. But the lasting one that carried the most power was seeing my brother's face and hearing my own plea. Over and over, the memory played in a loop, reminding me of a moment just seconds before everything had been taken from me.

The memory still plagued me with nightmares, as I imagined it would for some time. One did not get their mind rewritten with fake memories, have the real ones reappear, and not feel traumatized by it. It was a fate that was almost worse. Some days I still battled with which emotion lingered from it: fear or anger.

Suddenly, I dropped to the grass below the curved driveway. My hands pressed into the ground as I tried to calm my breathing. It was only a matter of seconds before I felt the warmth of Liam's hands on my face.

"Emma, love…look at me."

My eyes lifted to his bright gaze of deep worry before he leaned his forehead against mine. He didn't lecture me for ignoring his initial worry about staying in the room minutes ago. He merely sat patiently, letting me inhale his strength.

"I'm sorry…" I said almost breathlessly. "It's just the memory of that day…"

I could hardly finish my sentence. Fear was climbing its way up, making a worthy competitor for the anger simmering below the surface.

"I hate that you're still suffering," Liam said with a slightly angry quiver to his voice that I had never heard before.

"Deciding to be with you always meant accepting the possibility of danger."

I paused with a humorless exhale as my eyes zoned out of focus.

"But losing my memories of you is something I could never accept...not again." I was attempting to hold back tears but I knew my effort was unsuccessful when Liam used his thumbs to wipe the wetness off my cheeks. "And yet I'm scared every day they will be."

Liam stood, my body following like a magnet before his arms pulled me against him. I wrapped my arms tightly around him, turning my face into the warmth of his neck as he placed a kiss on the top of my head.

"I won't let that happen," Liam said.

I wasn't sure how long we stood there before the silent sanctuary was disturbed.

"I never meant to hurt you, Ems."

I stepped back from Liam as my neck turned at the unexpected voice I had known all my life. Suddenly, the fear was pulled down by the leg, making room for the anger to break free.

"And yet that's all you did," I said.

The twin serpent of anger had battled its way back to the surface, subduing the fear indefinitely. His timing was already misjudged and as soon as Sean attempted to reach forward with his own plea, I was lost to new fury.

"Ems, if you could just see it from—"

"Don't!"

My voice had scared an animal resting in the high trunk of the tree to my left. Thankfully, I had no immortal strength to add to the anger, to prevent me from simply snapping the large oak tree in the yard of the Alexander Mansion.

"Just because we're all dealing with Thomas doesn't mean I'm ready to hear you *explain*. I can't even stomach looking at you right now."

"Just give her some space," Liam advised.

"Once again, Liam, I don't need your advice. I'm not the only one to—"

"Stop right there, Sean." Both of them looked back at me. "You don't get to blame him for your choices."

"You were miserable!"

Sean stepped forward, gaining the inches toward me that I wished to avoid.

"I couldn't stand by and watch you wither any longer. Not when I could take it all away."

My throat felt as if it were closing in as I looked toward the ground. I couldn't take the breaking of his voice any longer. I shook my head, backing away.

"That was my pain to have, my love to remember. And you just robbed my soul of it without a second's thought."

I glanced up to see Sean's lips parting but no words came out. It was my moment to escape the conversation I could no longer bear.

"And yes, I will inevitably forgive you. Of course I will."

His lips curved for a moment before dropping at the image he was already picturing from my mind.

"Yeah," I said, nodding. "That moment of you in my room still haunts my dreams. I can still hear my pathetic pleas. So, yes, you will earn my forgiveness with time. It's inevitable." I shrugged, accepting my own truth. "But you will never be able to make me forget the betrayal of that day. Because your intentions left a mark. And I'll carry that scar on my heart for the rest of my life."

I turned on my heel, heading back toward the mansion, leaving him behind as I fought back my tears in silent agony.

CHAPTER 9

BURDEN TO BEAR

Later that evening, as I waited for Liam to return from his Watch, I found myself mindlessly covering the perimeter of his room. My methodical steps may have appeared calm on the outside but beneath my eyes, even a stranger could detect that the anxiety matched someone with a frantic pace.

It was a habit I had taken to while he was *on duty*. An anxiety I knew I would always internally battle for the rest of my life. Especially with all we had been through with our separation and his faked death. When you added Thomas's looming threat, I knew I had enough life material to write my own book series.

I adjusted the chain on my locket, sighing with satisfaction at its arrangement against my chest. As my hand dropped to my side, I noticed something white in between the nightstand and Liam's bed frame. I bent down, one hand resting on my knee as I reached forward with the other. I used my middle and index fingers to inch close enough to finally pull the folded paper into my full grasp. It was a regular piece of notebook paper that had fallen into the forgotten territory.

I unfolded it curiously before immediately grinning down at the handwriting that I knew so well. My own.

Jane Austen

Emily Bronte

William Shakespeare

It was the assignment from the first day of class last year. The day when Liam and I met. My grin turned to a full smile as my eyes were drawn to the writing near the bottom of the page. It was some of Liam's suggestions, which I later found out had been his four most recent novel conquests at the time. All of them rested on the wall-to-wall bookshelves in his bedroom.

Baroness Orczy- Scarlet Pimpernel

Murasaki Shikibu- The Tale of Genji

D. H. Lawrence- The Fox

Daphne du Maurier- Rebecca

I read each name with amusement, knowing I had devoured them from the very shelf that was feet away. I never imagined finding someone who read more than Sean and I did, and yet Liam proved he was ahead in that race. Of course, he had the advantage of two centuries.

Funny enough, I had always wondered what happened to the note that I now held in my hand. It seemed like another lifetime as I recalled the memory of putting away the note to listen to Mrs. Anderson. At the moment, I had assumed I would study it later, when I wasn't distracted by Liam's presence. Unfortunately, there wasn't a day after that when I *wasn't* distracted by him. That was probably why I never realized—or cared—that I had lost the paper.

It was sweet that Liam not only found and kept the shared note but must have recently been reliving the memory of our first interaction. My cheeks rose blissfully to the memory that had started it all. I pulled open the rightstand drawer and placed the escaped nostalgia back inside its likely home.

However, my smile suddenly disappeared as I forgot the enjoyment of the light-hearted assignment. My hand dropped the notebook paper as my attention shifted to a white envelope with Liam's handwriting.

Emma

Seeing my name in black ink forced my stomach to sink with heaviness. My gut instinct knew that hidden envelopes were rarely of a happy nature.

The very touch of this envelope sent a shiver down my spine. I contemplated how long it had lain solitarily in the drawer. The last letter I had received from Liam had arrived after I thought he had died. Even that letter still haunted me and the trepidation of this one caused my hands to shake.

I flipped it over and noticed that the seal had been tucked under, making it so that I wouldn't have to struggle to open it. Why I paid attention to that detail, I wasn't sure. Maybe because the small focus of Liam's consideration took away some of the fear.

I looked down at the envelope for what felt like hours—though I knew it was only minutes—before I found the courage to flip the seal with my right index finger and thumb.

I pulled the discolored paper out of the envelope with delicacy, as if expecting the content to explode. My body couldn't seem to relax, as the tension caused my heart to race and adrenaline to course through my veins.

I closed my eyes to help gain control of my increased breaths before allowing myself to unfold the letter. My nerves were standing on edge, the fear wrapping around my vital organs like a snake, suffocating them with a pressure I couldn't get to release.

Emma,

It feels odd to start a letter with a thank you but how can I not thank the sun for beaming down light after years of only shadow?

I gripped the paper as if trying to brace myself through the quiet stillness that misled you before the rising tsunami.

And yet, I know coveting such a gift is selfish. I may crave it but the sun was not built for me alone. It is meant for its own path and I am just one stop on that journey.

I could see the pen mark had begun to darken, as if it had been harder for him to write than it was for me to continue reading.

It was never fair of me to draw your affection when you are meant to live a normal life, a peaceful life, a fulfilled life. A life free of the danger that my family and I will inevitably draw closer to you, like a bow to an arrow. I could never continue my existence knowing that I was the one to cause the end of yours.

As the ink darkened once more, I could sense the pressure he must have been placing on the pen, as if trying to imprint the pain on the object itself. I couldn't help but wonder how many attempts he had made to sit down and finish the letter.

I took a deep breath, already feeling the lightness of the drops that were about to crash down from my eyes.

This is why it is with deep sorrow that I must part from you before my strength is overcome by the weakness of my desire. Though it causes an ache beneath my chest, it is what is best for you. All that matters is knowing you will continue to be in this world. For if not, what I do is meaningless.

I felt an ache throb beneath my chest as my throat began to painfully dry with each swallow. But I had to continue.

In time, just as the wind forgets the very grass it sweeps over in the abandoned meadows and fields, you also will forget the sound of my name and the sound of my voice. It is soon that I plead for the mercy of this, to avoid you feeling any thought of pain by my absence.

The storm could no longer be held back. My eyes released the drops like synchronized swimmers.

You must know that with each beat underneath my chest, that which reminds me of what I am, I will not forget the impression upon my heart you have left and will always make.

Please forgive me and know that even long after you have forgotten the very name that binds me, I will continue to carry the memory of your love until the end of my days.

With Love,

Liam

I didn't remember moving, but by the time my mind came back to take in my surroundings, I realized I was seated on the edge of Liam's bed. With fear in my throat, I heard the angelic voice behind me.

"I never meant for you to read that."

I stood, turning swiftly to find Liam leaning against the doorframe. His arms were crossed to mask the uncertainty beneath his bright emerald gaze.

"No?"

There was a challenge within my uneven tone.

"At least not after a certain point," Liam said.

He sighed, moving his eyes to the letter I held firmly within my hand before shifting his focus back on me.

"I knew from the moment we met, I was in trouble. But you just had this..." He paused as if still trying to understand our connection. "This pull that I couldn't ignore. I knew I shouldn't and yet I just had to be around you." He shrugged with a simultaneous shake of his head. "Deep down, I didn't need Sean to tell me it couldn't work. I knew it was wrong and I had to let go…let you be."

With each word, he stepped closer into the room, not once taking his gaze off of mine.

"It took me days to finish but once I signed my name, I knew I had to act that same day. I decided I would leave it and then rightfully disappear from your life."

I did my best to hide any expression but my mind winced at the irony of Liam writing a letter on Valentine's Day to officially tell me that we could not be together.

"But you were there in my room," I said, confirming my memory.

"I'd made my decision that morning, planning it out perfectly. I'd simply leave the note upon your bed and leave."

Though I didn't speak, I gazed back with a narrow mix of confusion and curiosity.

"But when the moment came, I couldn't will myself to let go of the letter." Liam paused, his eyes swimming in the memory, as if still stumped by the outcome. "I was unaware of how long I'd been hesitating until I heard you arrive home." He shook his head in disbelief. "And suddenly, despite my capability, my body froze as if convincing myself I needed to see you one last time before letting go."

Both of us were quite aware that his telekinetic ability would have allowed him to deliver the letter without needing to be *in* my room. And yet—

"It's foolish now to think that I would ever have had the strength at all." He exhaled with a small grin despite the humorless tone. "It was selfish and unwise to stay but—"

"Why do you still have it?"

He was silent, moving toward me with a cautious step.

"I don't know."

"Is it still something you think about?"

"I think about the consequence of that choice every day," he said with a small tilt of his head.

"It's too late to be an option," I said.

"It will never *not* be an option, Emma."

I stepped around the bed until I was inches from him. Quickly, I reached up to hold his face. My thumb moved against his cheek as we gazed at each other.

"It's an option only if you can tell me that you don't love me."

He lifted his palms to place the warmth over my own before his forehead leaned against mine.

"I'll never stop loving you, Emma."

I pulled my head back, still feeling a hesitation that shot through his body and into his words.

"Tell me what's really bothering you then."

He stood silent, trying to resist the need to describe the inner struggle, despite my knowing it was here. I watched a small grin surface at the thought of me knowing him so well. He moved his hands so that he could use his thumbs to softly wipe away the remaining wetness on my face.

"You know I'd give you anything on this earth that you wanted. But..." He was looking at me with heavy, despair-filled eyes. "...but I'll never be able to give you children."

I was taken aback by the confession, unprepared for that topic to be the reason for his unease. It didn't seem as if it would be a priority when with an immortal. Even my own subconscious knew to forget it. My family heirloom bracelet was proof of that.

What I held certainty on was that I wanted Liam and if the compromise was no children, I would happily take that deal. There was a chance I may never want children but I would always want Liam.

"That's it?" I asked with eased curiosity.

Liam's eyes flew up as if he were thrown off by the nonchalance of my words.

"Not having the choice to have children is not something any woman should have to go through. But it's the one thing I could never give you and that isn't fair to ask of you. You should be able to have as many as you want."

He turned his back to me as he made his way over to sit on the edge of his bed, folding his head into his hands.

I instinctively gravitated toward him, pulling his hands away and holding each side of his face with ease.

"I don't need children, Liam," I said firmly.

I covered his lips with my finger to silence the disagreement arising.

"Liam, I'm not even certain I'd want children. Nowadays, it's hard to be certain of anything except one thing."

"What's that?"

"You," I said.

He looked up in a half-smile that I returned, before glancing off to the side. I leaned my head forward, pressing my forehead to his in comfort, letting him entwine his hands in my hair.

"You say that now but what about when you're in your 60s and you resent me for it?"

"When I'm 60, I'll have you. If I don't have *you*, then I'll never want anything."

He looked down but I used my hand to raise his chin to me. Liam refused to look at me but he placed his right arm around my back, needing me closer.

"Every woman should have the option of being able to have children. I can't let you give that up so easily. Not when you'll hate me in 50 years once your opportunity has flown by."

"Is that what you really think?"

He finally glanced up at me while my thumb moved with comfort against his cheekbone.

"Liam, do you not realize the love I have for you?"

I exhaled heavily, frustrated. I wanted him to not only hear my words but feel the truth of them.

"I'll love you from the first day until my last day. That means I don't want a child with someone else if it means I don't get you."

"But you could do that. Because you have every right to conceive a child even if I'm not the father."

"But I don't *want* to carry a child that isn't yours."

"Not right now. But one day you might feel that desire."

I sighed with frustration. There was no way to prove this to him without traveling into our future. I leaned my forehead to his and closed my eyes. We weren't finished, but there were no more words we could say. I'd just have to help him see that children weren't in our future and I'd never resent him for that.

I positioned myself in his lap with my arms around his neck as he shifted my body and legs around his own. Liam closed his arms around my waist before I laid my head to his collarbone. I closed my eyes and he leaned his cheek to rest atop my head as he inhaled the scent of my hair.

"You say this as if you'll always be so certain."

His words had come out in almost a whisper.

"That's because I know how I feel about you. It's irrevocable."

I could feel the light kiss he placed on my temple.

"Isn't this all premature, anyway? We don't even know if I'll survive to see graduation."

It was meant as a joke but as I pulled back, I could see his jaw clench. For the first time, it felt as if I were talking to Sean. Liam's mood was not lighthearted in any way.

"I've never even mentioned children before so where did this even come from?"

Liam looked down and played with the bracelet around my wrist.

"Sean told me about the meaning behind your bracelet," Liam said.

I sighed, feeling the heaviness of my breath. I lifted my head back to meet his eyes, feeling the connection flow through us. I knew that there was no way to show him. All I could do was tell him and hope that was enough.

"You have to let me make my own choices."

I cupped his cheek with my right palm and held his gaze.

"So if you don't want to put that burden on yourself, then don't. It's mine to bear. In the end, it's not Sean's or even your decision."

I paused, watching his eyes brighten with an alluring pull.

"It's mine," I said, pointing to my chest.

I leaned down to meet the soft, tender lips I would be lucky to kiss for the rest of my days.

"I'll be by your side as long as you want me," Liam said.

I exhaled, truly grateful for the beautiful soul that had come into my life. I pulled back, gazing into the bright green that studied me. I reached out to hold the side of his face, grinning as he leaned into my touch. Words would never be enough to describe how much I truly loved him.

"That makes two of us."

CHAPTER 10

HOPE

My new strapless lavender dress fit me perfectly with its unique feathered fluff design. Lillian had even provided me with a matching clutch and a pair of designer heels. I lightly touched my hair, which was pulled up halfway with clips, leaving the other section slightly curled as it hung in front of my collarbone.

It had been two weeks since that terrible night on the boat. My survival instinct felt as if it was constantly screaming for me to quarantine myself from events that would leave me exposed. But my rational side knew that life had to remain as it had always been. That was the whole point of Jane's request, after all. If I didn't put myself into a risky situation and continue with the charade of a normal routine, we would be no closer to confronting Thomas—and no closer to this all being over.

Plus, I had to admit that I was a bit eager to be put in a situation that forced Michael to finally talk to me. I nodded silently at the thought as my red fingernail traced the white calligraphy on the rustic-style invitation in my hand:

MR. AND MRS. KEVIN MILLER &
MR. JAMES HARRIS
REQUEST THE HONOR OF YOUR PRESENCE
AT THE MARRIAGE OF THEIR CHILDREN
PAIGE LEIGH
TO
MATTHEW CHARLES HARRIS
SATURDAY, THE THIRD OF MARCH
TWO THOUSAND AND TWELVE AT HALF PAST
THREE IN THE AFTERNOON

"Are you ready?" my mom asked as she stepped from around the corner. Her auburn hair was styled up, showing the natural beauty of her high cheekbones and hazel eyes. I glanced down to see the black stilettos Grace had "sent her in the mail" for Christmas, which paired well with the stunning knee-length hunter green cocktail dress she was wearing. I smiled only to realize, as I looked up, that she must have been doing the same of me and my own outfit.

"I'm ready," I said.

The ceremony lasted half an hour. Then we found ourselves pulling up to the outside reception, where a DJ was already playing music. I followed my mom to one of the open-seated round tables that were placed in an arrangement encircling the wooden dance floor.

We had been seated for ten minutes when the groomsmen made their entrance. My gaze found Michael's. Surprisingly, he diverted from the group and headed straight for me. I quickly stood, grateful my mom was elsewhere, talking with Josh and Janet Wood.

"Hey," I said.

"Hey," Michael repeated.

He sat in my mom's seat and I naturally followed his movement by sitting back in my own. I looked down for a few seconds, pretending to smooth out my dress despite it being perfectly steamed by Lillian herself.

"How have you been?"

I cringed at the small talk we had to float through in order to get over the awkwardness of the past two months.

"Well, I made it through the hard part, so..." he said with a raised brow as he looked around the outside venue of his brother's wedding.

"Yeah. Speaking of that, aren't you supposed to be sitting with them?" I said, pointing to the long, white-covered table where the other groomsmen and bridesmaids sat. A few were throwing glances our way.

"I'm good here." He teasingly shrugged, holding the crooked smirk I knew well. "Besides, what are they going to do? Throw me out of the wedding for breaching seating protocol?"

I rolled my eyes but couldn't help chuckling as my mom approached the table.

"Well, don't you look dashing?"

"I have to make an effort sometimes," Michael said as he stood in order to hug my mother.

Mom naturally moved her hand to his face with a nurturing understanding within her smile.

"Alyssa would have been very proud of the gentlemen you turned out to be."

Michael nodded. "I know that Matt wishes she could have been here."

"You can't see her but she is," my mom said.

"I hope so," Michael said.

Before another word could be spoken, our attention was turned toward the introduction of Paige and Matt, who were walking into the reception. They both positively glowed as they started in on their first dance.

Just as others were invited to join them on the dance floor, Uncle Greg made his way to our table. I looked at my mother's beaming smile as he pulled back the open chair next to her. I turned away with a twitch of my lips, as if I were the only one enjoying the inside joke of their skinny love.

I hadn't realized I was in my own thoughts until Michael cleared his throat. He held out his palm with a bow of his head. Despite the way he mocked himself, there was an underlying chivalry that warmed me as he reached for my hand.

"Would you like to dance?"

"I'd love to," I said as he pulled me to my feet.

"Right this way, then."

Once on the dance floor, he stopped and swung me around to face him. My hands automatically fell into place on his right shoulder and left hand but I wasn't sure if that was by design or by my own readied instinct.

"Smooth," I said.

"I'm very smooth, so don't ruin it by stepping on my feet."

"You just watch it with the spins," I said.

His smile was wide and I knew without a doubt that he was going to dramatically spin me. Through my laughter, I was grateful the awkwardness had quickly faded between us and we could just enjoy the night.

"I'm signing with Georgia next week."

"Really?"

He nodded, clearly trying his best to contain the excitement that came from the accomplishment.

"That's so exciting! I guess I'll have to start cheering for Georgia now."

"As if you were watching a lot of baseball to begin with."

"Fair point but I have a reason now," I said.

"I'll be sure to send you some Bulldog swag."

"Obviously," I said, rolling my eyes in a teasing manner.

There was a moment of silence as Michael seemed to be trying to collect his courage. My guard was already getting its defenses back in place.

"So…how's Liam?"

"He's good."

"Emma, don't get mad, okay?" He paused to tilt his head in a position to look at me. "We're just talking."

"Okay…"

He must have been waiting for the permission of my words before he could convince himself to start once more.

"I just need to know for my own peace of mind…"

"Michael," I warned.

"I never would have left you the way he did."

"Aren't you leaving for Georgia after we graduate?" I said, hoping the truth of my words would easily dismantle this conversation completely.

His mouth opened and I realized that the teasing angle had been the wrong choice.

"Yeah but that doesn't mean—"

"I'm with Liam," I said bluntly.

"So you never thought about what it would have been like if we'd tried?"

I closed my eyes with a deep sigh, frustrated by more than just the conversation. He had no idea of the implanted memories I still carried when we *were* together. He had no idea that I *did* know what it was like because it was forced upon us like two lab rats. But despite Sean and Patrick's experiment, my heart belonged to only one person in the real world.

I chewed at my bottom lip, hating the reality of the harsh moment—mostly because I knew I couldn't avoid hurting him with the truth. And yet I had to find a way to make him understand. It was the last thing I wanted to do but it was inevitable if I wanted to mend our friendship.

"Michael, why can't you see it?"

His brow furrowed in confusion and I internally moaned in slight annoyance at the confrontation.

"This isn't a love triangle," I said, pointing between himself and me. "There are no teams to side with, no tough choice to make between two people." I hated every moment of my speech and yet it had come to a point of needing to be expressed. Enough was enough. It was time to accept or move on. "Because there is and always will be one person whom I love."

"Okay, I get it," Michael mumbled.

"Do you?"

It wasn't a question to be cruel but to clarify.

"You love Liam."

"Yes, and I hate that the idea makes you hurt. I'd never wish that for you. I want you in my life more than anything but I need you to understand that first. Someone else has my heart and they always will. Not accepting that is a deal-breaker."

"I'm sorry," Michael said in a defeated voice.

"You don't have to apologize—"

He cut me off, halting our movement completely. "But I am. I realized now that it's unfair to guilt you into anything. It's not your fault that you love him any more than it's my fault that I love you."

My smile was soft and kind but carried a pity I hoped he didn't see.

"I want you in my life, even if that means as friends. As long as you're happy, that's all that matters."

"Thank you," I said. "And I have no doubt that one day you're going to find someone who makes you forget about this.

Someone who'll carry your heart in a way you never thought possible, making you question what you ever felt for me."

"To hope," Michael said.

I nodded as our movements commenced on the dance floor.

"You could name your daughter that someday."

"Maybe," he said through a light chuckle before twirling me around again. As I turned, I saw Matt and his new bride. They held the same elated smiles that radiated adoration for each other. Matt leaned in to whisper something into Paige's ear, causing her to lightly pull his head closer with her hand, connecting their temples.

Suddenly I could feel Michael at my own ear with a soft tenderness.

"Thank you."

My head turned only slightly, not yet in his direction, as I waited for his voice to continue.

"For what?" I asked in a low voice that spoke to his shoulder.

"For being so kind."

I gulped, suddenly tilting back my head for the first time, staring into his baby blue eyes.

"I could say the same about you."

He grinned with a curious wonder in his gaze.

"Liam's a lucky guy."

My eyes moved back and forth with his own, as if I were trying to find the mature man who was controlling the boy in front of me.

"We both got lucky there."

So many things rushed to my mind, but nothing could reach my lips as I turned my head back over his shoulder and away from his gaze.

He must have noticed my eyes on the beautiful essence that was Paige in her flowing white silk spaghetti strap gown. There was a natural glow within her cheeks. But there was something about it that I couldn't quite figure out and couldn't seem to look away from either.

"I'm sure you'll carry the same glow when the day comes."

"Wait, she's..." My brow furrowed but my thoughts were interrupted by Michael's next words.

"Pregnant, yes." It wasn't a gossip-like tone but more matter-of-fact. And low enough for no one around to hear. "They haven't told anyone except Dad and me."

It was as if my mind had waited for those words. All the signs came out, bleeding from the walls, as if they had been exposed the whole time, invisible to my observation. I saw the way she occasionally moved her right hand to her abdomen, the way Matt looked happily toward her stomach with pride, causing her returned elation, and the way she had gracefully denied anything but water.

I smiled as I gazed between the two newlyweds and their soon-to-be addition. In a time when nothing seemed certain, it was nice to raise a mental toast to us all.

To hope.

CHAPTER 11

Ready or Not

I took off my heels and heard the mental sigh of relief from my arches as they sank into the carpet. I was pulling on a pair of sweatpants and grabbing a shirt when I heard a message alert from my phone.

I walked over to my bed while pulling my loose-fitting V-neck over my head. When I grabbed the phone from my bed, I was pleasantly surprised to see it was a text from Michael.

Left you something on the porch.

I walked over to my bedroom window and peeked through the closed blinds. My brow rose in wrinkled confusion.

Just now? I typed back.

I waited patiently as the bubbles appeared on my screen to show that he was typing.

Yep.

I shook my head as I texted, Why didn't you knock, weirdo?

Couldn't stay long. Wanted you to know it was there. I began to type only to be interrupted by another message from him. Didn't want you to leave it out there in case it rained or something.

Fair enough, I quickly typed back even though I knew our porch was deep enough to protect whatever it was he had left for me. Not to mention, both of us knew there was no sight of a cloud that would suggest rain.

But instead of teasing, I simply wrote, I'll go grab it!

What a load off, Michael sent back.

I rolled my eyes before throwing my phone on the bed once again. Just as I was about to reach for my door, I heard a knock from the other side.

"Come in," I said.

The knob turned slowly, revealing my mom, who popped her head through the crack of the opening with a smile, then pushed the open door at the sight of me. Unlike me, she had yet to change out of her dress but was at least comfortably barefoot as she entered my room.

"Good timing," I said. "I was just heading your way."

"That is good timing," she said.

It was hard to resist the light that radiated off my mother when she entered a room. She was like a sun that brightened your mood when she was near, and most days that left me feeling undeserving.

"This was on the porch for you," she said while shifting her arms to reveal a large black box wrapped with a powder blue bow. "The card was knocked off a few feet but I picked it up too."

"Oh, wow," I said, pulling my head back in surprise.

"Who's it from?" my mom asked.

"Michael just sent me a text a few minutes ago, saying that he left something." I took the package from her hands, watching her raised suspicion. "I had no idea it would be so..."

"Extravagant."

"That's one way to word it," I said.

I bit the inside of my cheek, practically hearing the amusement already inside Sean's head.

"That's all you need."

"What?"

It was only at my mother's response that I realized I had said the mumbled sarcastic words aloud. I turned to place the box on the bed while looking back over my shoulder.

"Would you mind if I opened it alone?"

"Sure, babe."

I expected a slight hurt tone to occupy her voice but thankfully was met with an understanding smile.

"I'll tell you about it later," I said with an appreciative grin.

"You got it," she said with a wink before shutting the door behind her.

I opened the card hastily, careful not to cut myself because of my eagerness. I pulled out the card, looking at the cute puppy with a bouquet of flowers in its mouth. There was a bubble above the Labrador's head that said, *I'm sorry.* Upon opening the apology card, I recognized Michael's handwriting.

Emma,

Believe it or not, I have had this card for a while but have been waiting to have the guts to get over my own pride and give it to you. Anyway, I just wanted you to know that I miss you too. And I'm sorry for being a jerk and cutting you off like that.

You didn't do anything wrong and it wasn't fair of me to blame you for falling in love with someone who isn't me. And I don't want to be the kind of person who kicks people out of his life because he can't handle not getting loved back. Because not having you in my life at all seems a far worse punishment. So I hope you can forgive me and let us be friends again.

Love,

Michael

I held a lopsided grin before reaching down to pull at the blue ribbon until it allowed me to completely slide off the top of the black box. Once I tossed aside the lid and parted the tissue paper, I felt unprepared for what waited for me inside. I lifted out a red knee-length, one-shoulder chiffon dress with a ruffled bodice. Underneath lay a pair of black stilettos and a black satin clutch bag with a crystal-designed buckle.

What the hell? I thought.

I reached for my phone and typed out a message to Michael as I looked down at the dress still in my hands. **This was really sweet but you didn't have to do all this.**

Really? How else do you apologize if not with an "I'm sorry" card?

My head was tilted in protest, still not comfortable accepting it all but I couldn't resist teasing back with my message.

Does that make red the apology color, then?

The bubbles on my screen formed and disappeared twice before he finally decided on what to respond with. The flowers little Benji is holding are yellow, dork. Please tell me you haven't gone colorblind in our time apart.

I'm talking about the dress color, you jerk. Most definitely RED.

Wait. Michael's message had an ellipsis before it ended with, What dress?

The one inside the black box you left me. Though I was mostly grateful to be having this conversation through text message, the one drawback was not being able to hear his voice. By his tone, I would have known in seconds if he was teasing me.

Are you being serious?

Are you? I typed back.

Emma, all I left was the card.

Reading him say my name made my arms stiffen. It was something he would write only to emphasize that he was being serious. Despite my unease, I instinctively knew I had to play it off as a joke. I still had to figure out who *really* left the dress and I didn't need to add Michael's new concern to that.

I'm just kidding, I typed with a smiling emoji before making sure to acknowledge the sweet note he *did* leave me. And of course we can still be friends. I'd love nothing more.

I threw down my phone as I tried to rationalize it. Had Lillian dropped by and forgotten to tell me? It was her territory, after all, but she didn't usually deliver her gifted outfits in a box. And she always left me a little note with the outfit if she did.

I went back to the box, flipping it over until all the contents dumped out onto my bed. My shoulders slumped and my lips scrunched to the side at seeing the absence of any note. At least that was until I looked at the lid of the box, which had been carelessly tossed aside. My new focus could see a folded cream-colored piece of stationery taped on the inside of the lid.

"Clever, Lil," I said to myself as I reached down and pulled the note away from the tape. But as my eyes met the handwriting, I knew instantly that it wasn't from Lillian.

I thought these would look stunning on you. I look forward to the moment I get to see for myself.

-Thomas

I dropped the note as if the material had burned my skin. My eyes studied the gifts on my bed with caution, certain they were equal to the danger of an angered cobra.

It wasn't until I heard the small tap on my window that I realized I wasn't alone. I looked up to see the echoed concern radiating off Liam's bright green eyes.

Though I wanted to move, I couldn't find the motivation to get my legs to obey me. Luckily, that didn't matter with my telekinetic boyfriend. Within seconds of my hesitation, I watched my bedroom window rise before he agilely jumped through and made his way over to me.

"Are you alright?"

Unsure of how to answer, I merely wrapped my arms around him, pressing my face into the warmth of his chest. The feel of his kiss to my head released a calming sedative into my bloodstream. Finally, after a few long minutes, I was able to look up at him.

We didn't need words to express the fear that came from the expected inevitable first contact with Thomas. Maybe we both naively hoped for the best but the incident on the boat should have told us differently. Thomas's gift was quite clear: We had already started playing a game whether or not we were ready.

From the moment Liam had taken me from my room to join the Alexanders at the mansion, there was an uneasy silence.

"How certain are we that Jane hasn't played us? That it wasn't her intention from the beginning?"

William was normally the Alexander in the group who quietly listened with calm observation. But hearing his concern vocalized was unsettling, to say the least.

"Will makes a good point," Lillian said. "Who's to say her plan wasn't to just lead us all into a trap this whole time? Grace, did you gauge her when she was here?"

"I felt pain and anger from her but any one of us in this room would exude that type of emotion if we were dealing with the loss of not one but two of us." Grace shrugged. "Nothing abnormal to me."

"I trust her," I said before anyone else could speak. It was hard to know if it was meant to be addressed to the group of immortals or to myself.

All bright eyes turned to me, carrying an incredulous gaze that the sacrificed target was the one to back Jane.

"I know I'm the odd one out here, as a human, but when she requested my help for her plan, it felt entirely genuine." I sighed, making time to focus on each Alexander as I spoke. "And besides, she clearly warned us that she was going to look bad to keep Thomas's trust." I watched the acknowledging nods from William and Lillian as I continued. "Remember, she told us that if she was doing her job right, it would look like she wasn't on our side. Why should we doubt that now?"

"She's right," Liam said. "Jane has never given us a reason to not trust her on this plan. She has the personality of a frigid cat." Lillian and Grace let out a simultaneous chuckle at Liam's truthful words. "But she's also one of the most honor-bound immortals I know. It would be unlike her to go against her word."

"Like Henry was honor-bound," Lillian challenged.

"We have to stop comparing them. It's not fair to judge the entire coven by the actions of one," I said.

"Why is it that the human here is the rational one?" William said before winking at me.

"Let's just remember when we agreed to this that we all knew the risk." I folded my arms across my chest as if that would boost the confidence of my words. "And I know that sounds strange coming from the bait itself but even I know this is about more than me. It's about all of the people you were created to protect."

I looked around with hopeful eyes, somewhat embarrassed about my pleading attempt at motivation.

"Well, if she's in, then so am I," Lillian said, stepping forward with a prideful smile.

"Me too," Grace said with a small nod.

"You have my vote, little Morgan," William said as he took Lillian's hand in his own.

"Us too," Patrick and Mary said in unison.

I looked over at Liam, who held an adoring stare, his next words just above a whisper. "I'm always with you." It was as if he were speaking only to me despite knowing the others could hear him quite well.

"And you?"

At Patrick's voice, I looked up, bouncing my eyes over to where his gaze fell. Sean entered the room, absorbing every pair of eyes that fell upon him but looking at nothing but the space in front of him.

Strangely, he remained silent but reciprocated with a single nod of agreement—one that signified that the plan would continue. We were all in and would see it through until whatever the end might be.

CHAPTER 12

Grateful Consequence

The next day I could hear small laughter coming from the kitchen as I made my way into my house. Though I already knew where she was, instinct called out to my mom anyway.

"Mom?"

There was a slight pause and a small screech from one of the kitchen chairs, as if her body had positioned itself in my direction while remaining seated.

"In here!"

I walked around, expecting to find the familiar sight of my uncle occupying the middle kitchen table chair. But my feet froze in step, my checks dropping simultaneously with the upward pull of my chest at the man who turned in his seat.

He was dressed in a grey cardigan worn over a white button-up shirt and blue striped tie. The familiar outfit surfaced quickly in my memory, as the cardigan had been an item he often wore while teaching. Most in Washington had come to know him as Mr. Sutton but I had the unfortunate experience of knowing better.

"Thomas," I breathed out in an inaudible whisper.

As the immortal turned his head in my direction, I saw that his face was framed with the same pair of glasses he wore as a substitute teacher. He pretended to fidget with them while revealing the hidden grey eyes brightness of his eyes, if only for a moment, to remind me of the control he held in my own kitchen.

But even when the color of his eyes hibernated back into the disguise of a human likeness, the curl of his lips was more terrifying. I was eager to look at my mother but didn't want to give Thomas any reason to have her attention. Instead, I remained frozen with an unrelenting gaze on the immortal, trying to calm my breathing and yet feeling unsuccessful every time my chest constricted.

"You must be Emma," Thomas said.

"Yes," I said in a low volume of reluctance.

At my reaction, he tilted his head and revealed his teeth in a satisfied smile. I mentally scolded myself for playing into the fear. But whether he knew if that fear was for me was hard to tell. My lips pulled inward. I hated that, once again, someone was in the crossfire of danger because they knew me. I felt frustrated and helpless about the position I had put my mother in despite knowing that it wasn't my fault.

Pushing past the suit, I focused on the moment for what it was. The Alexanders and I had talked last night about how Thomas would expect me to run to them for protection after the arrival of his gift. It would also be inevitable for him to make a power move by revealing himself in person, like he would need to prove a point about his control. Of course, knowing the plan didn't make my joints any less stiff or my throat any less dry.

He stood and my body tensed as he stepped closer, lifting his hand to introduce—or reintroduce—himself. His stare was an invitation for me to expose him to my mother, who had no inclination of the discomfort I was radiating into the room.

"I'm Alexander Lewis."

Already, his brow twitched in amusement at the sight of my tense jaw. The tension was carried down to my stomach at the fake name that came from his lips. The taunt of using Liam's combined human and immortal names seemed to give Thomas a heightened non-drug-infused high.

"But you can call me Alex," he continued.

I looked over at my mom, quickly realizing that apparently not everyone *did* know him as Mr. Sutton.

"Mr. Lewis here..." My mom paused as Thomas looked back at her, causing her to hold up her hands in a gestured apology. "Sorry, *Alex* is new to Washington and I volunteered to show him around."

Finally, my mom detected the tension on my face but she was picking up on the wrong conclusion. It was clear she thought I was irritated by another male figure being in my father's home. And though I felt a little guilty of that, I knew a way to manipulate her own guilt into getting him out of the house. I squinted my eyes suspiciously, playing up my false pretense.

"Our house doesn't seem like much of a tour of Washington," I said coldly.

"Emma," my mother said warningly, in a tone I hadn't heard her use in years.

"Your mother found me lost while grocery shopping and kindly invited me over for some sweet tea," Thomas explained with a fake charming innocence.

What the hell was my mother thinking? Who invites someone they don't know, let alone a *man* they don't know, back to their house? Southern hospitality should have its limits.

"I should be going," Thomas said, looking between the two of us. "I have so much unpacking to do anyway. Thank you for being so kind, Angelia."

My mom looked as if she wanted to protest before shifting her gaze over to me with remorse. My stomach twisted but ultimately the guilt trip had worked.

"It was my pleasure, Alex. Next time you'll have to meet my brother-in-law and my son."

Thomas began walking toward the door as he spoke with a nod of intrigue.

"Yes, I'd love to meet them both." He paused, turning to gaze back at me, revealing once again the bright immortal glow of his eyes.

"I hope to see you again real soon," Thomas said with a curled twist of his lip that my mother couldn't see. "And good luck with those college admissions. I'll keep my fingers crossed for Stanford."

By the time he looked up at my mom's polite smile, the color of his eyes was back to the camouflage he possessed. That very gift made it clear how he had been a threat for so many centuries. Hard to see the bite coming from behind when you're looking for a threat only in front of you.

I stood silent as he turned and walked down the porch. I waited until my mom had fully shut the door before moving toward the hallway, mumbling vaguely about going to my room. I was all too grateful my mom didn't follow.

I closed the door to my room, then leaned back with my eyes closed, hoping my heart would slow. I knew right then that college decisions would have to take a back seat until this played out. Thomas was never going to let me forget that no place was safe because he would always find a way to get to me if he desired.

"Are you alright?"

I flinched, opening my eyes at the sight of Sean's concerned gaze.

"I'm fine," I said, pushing off the door.

"The hell you are."

The fight felt all too familiar and too close to a wound that had barely begun to scar.

"Alright, no, I'm not," I said with a frustrated breath. "But no normal person would be *fine* after that."

I walked over to my bed, running my fingers through my hair.

"Don't forget you agreed," I said.

We both knew there was no way out of the plan anymore. The weight of that had trapped us both in a helpless fear.

"I should have never asked Grace to help me with getting Dad transferred back here," Sean mumbled.

My shoulders rose in alert, turning to my brother with a furrowed brow. "Wait, we moved back because of you?"

He sighed, contemplating the best explanation for the words he had just spit out. Finally, he walked over and sat on the bed, the hazel honey glow of his eyes brightening even more.

"I know I shouldn't have interfered and now I wish I hadn't..." He paused, shaking his head in disappointment at the consequence. "I just wanted you to be happy again."

The guilt confession was like being handed a puzzle piece I hadn't realized I was missing. His fear and guilt bled together from a decision he had made to bring me back into his life—a decision whose consequences were drowning him.

I placed my hand over his, curling my fingers around the edge. My eyes looked up at the face of the one who had loved me and protected me for my entire life. I nodded as if I was finally understanding the reasoning behind his overprotective behavior, which had been heightened at the moment Liam and I met.

"Sean," I said, drawing his attention. "I know we're not *okay* yet. And this may not end how we thought but I need you to know that I'm grateful for what you did."

His eyes bounced back and forth, seeping up the truth of my words. I may not have been able to help the fear subside but I could let him know, unlike the memory wipe, that this was a decision I was grateful he made.

"Because of you, I *am* happy again."

The left side of his face twitched in an attempted smile as he brought his other hand to cover mine with his immortal warmth. I laid my head against his shoulder before he laid his cheek on top of it.

Suddenly it was as if my anger was lifting from my chest, being expelled from my body like a virus. All that was left was the desperate need to soak up these moments with my best friend. Especially when we didn't know how many we had left.

CHAPTER 13

Marked Target

I was breathing heavily from my run as I made my way up the front porch and into my house. I used the bottom of my shirt to wipe my face as I headed down the hallway and into my room.

I opened my dresser and grabbed a fresh cotton t-shirt and my favorite pair of black leggings, ready to throw them on the bed for when I got out of the shower. But I stopped once I noticed something lying on my bed—something I hadn't placed there when I left for my run.

I walked closer to find three brochures attached to three separate admissions applications. UNC, DUKE, and

STANFORD. I smiled, trying to guess whether my mom or Sean had snuck in and left them there for me to find. As I looked between them, I felt a hand squeeze my hip and a pair of lips placed inches from my ear in order to whisper with a lullaby tone.

"California dream…"

I turned suddenly, stepping away from the grasp that wasn't Liam's. My body stood frozen at the sight of Thomas's standing a few feet away with a teasing grin.

I could hear Jane's words in my head. *His obsession with you will be his downfall.* Would it, though, or would it be mine?

I backed toward my bed, feeling the fear pulse through my veins like a poison that didn't know how to escape. I stopped when my foot hit the edge of the bed but kept my eyes on the glowing grey pair of eyes studying me with amusement.

"What do you want?"

He stepped closer, reaching around until he held the Stanford brochure in his grasp.

"Almost time to start deciding on universities, no?"

"And you're here what…recruiting?"

He chuckled in an unnerving adoration of my sarcasm as he reached forward to play with a piece of my hair.

"I just want you to know that you can go as far as you like."

His hand rose, curving an index finger before tracing it along my check and across my lips. My eyelids fluttered, desperate to close and escape but unwilling to lose him from my sight.

He winked before his other hand pulled apart my shaking hands enough to slide the brochure into my grasp. I glanced down for just a second to see which of the three he had given me. STANFORD.

He lifted his palms to rest on each side of my face, softly outlining my skin with his thumbs.

"But I'll always find you, Emma."

"No!"

My torso rose, sweat beams barely starting to form as my mind fought off my reality. I felt a hand on my arm and it made me shoot off the bed.

"Get away from me," I shouted.

My breathing was heavy and the blinks only seemed to bring about more darkness until a light surfaced brightly in the room.

"Emma...Emma."

I shook my head, hearing Liam call to me, but the fear still trapped me inside my mind. At least until I felt a pair of familiar, soft lips press into mine, silencing the world and my mind with it.

"It's me, love. Emma, can you hear me?"

I blinked, focusing on Liam, who pulled back his neck while cupping my face with his hands. Finally, I was able to control my breath with normal inhalations as I took in the familiar glow of emerald looking back at me. My hands rose to rest on top of his.

"Liam," I said with relief.

"I'm here."

He lowered his lips to my forehead, watching as I simply nodded in appreciation, not quite able to vocalize my thoughts just yet.

"Is she alright?"

My body twitched at the other voices and I pulled into Liam for security. "It's just Mary and Patrick."

I knew that and yet my mind was still on alert as the two eldest Alexanders stood with worried brows near the end of Liam's bed.

"I'm sorry," I said, pulling away from Liam and looking up at each of them with embarrassment.

"No need to apologize," Patrick said as his eyes circled my face.

"Are you alright? Did you hurt yourself?"

The compassion carried through in Mary's words and in her small, cautious steps as she kneeled down to me. I shook my head but she reached out to check my body anyway.

"Thomas," I said.

All three heads snapped up at once, waiting for me to elaborate. After two weeks, it wasn't surprising for me to have nightmares but it was still alarming when they left me violently screaming when Thomas appeared in one of them.

"It was about..." I paused, switching away from the exact details and moving on to my theory of why I had the nightmare. "There's no going back for me on this."

"Emma," Liam said in an attempt to soothe me.

"No, listen..." I held up my hand, looking into Mary's blue gaze as I remembered her words the day we met. "I've signed on to ride this out to the end."

I looked over at the three near me and saw the realization hit them in waves. It was as if, in all the joking, we all finally believed

125

my idle fears. There was a real chance this plan would end exactly how Jane had unwantedly predicted.

Mary gazed toward the ground as if a memory was haunting her mind. Patrick nodded with a small grin as if trying to appease me with comfort but his eyes remained clouded in bright grief. We both knew he was far too wise to have not already been expecting such an outcome.

I turned away, my eyes moving heavily as if trying to resist the command until they focused on Liam. Together, we looked at one another as if unwillingly coming to the same conclusion.

"If I die…" The words seemed to trigger Liam, causing the tension of his jaw to spread down his neck and throughout his body while his hands curled swiftly into fists. My stomach clenched at the sight. I wasn't the only one who was slowly being forced to grasp the reality of my risk.

I walked closer until I was able to reach out and cup his face, soothing his cheek with my thumb. I knew he didn't like hearing me say it any more than I liked having to accept it. But I needed him to understand.

"Liam," I said as if I were calling to someone else trapped within the immortal body looking back at me. "I need you to hear me."

Finally, I could feel the release of his tension as he leaned into my touch. I breathed out an amount of air I hadn't realized I'd been holding onto. My next words echoed in my head, as I knew they would quickly find their way to the immortals who weren't in this room.

"If I die, don't let it be for nothing."

CHAPTER 14

Five-Year Deal

I hadn't realized where I was going until I was on 15th Street, pulling in front of the hunter green sign of *Linda's Flowers & Gifts*.

As I walked in, I immediately saw the warm grin from the familiar short-framed woman with long silver hair that rested below her rib cage. I had not seen Mrs. Rennert since my dad's funeral. Unfortunately, that meant her smile—although genuine—held a pitied edge. If only people understood that the empathic sadness they gave off, while laced with good intentions, only made the reality of losing someone that much harder.

I walked straight to the counter behind which she stood. Immediately, her stare made me uncomfortable. I commanded my eyes to look left and right before I allowed them to lift up to the patient brown eyes waiting for my gaze.

"What can I do for you today, Emma?"

Her voice was low, yet still cheerful.

"Do you have any white lilies?"

Her eyes widened and her hands clasped together with an excited sense of pride. She came across as the type to never be caught out of stock.

"Yes, I have some fresh ones in the back. How many do you need?"

She went to the back corner, looking at me as she readied herself.

"Just one, please."

She nodded and grabbed the long-stemmed white flower.

She placed it on the counter with a graceful pleasure. It was then that I noticed a bright orange lily sitting in a tall, clear vase near the register on the counter.

"That definitely stands out," I said, gesturing at the bright flower.

"Oh, yes. It's not a popular choice because of its meaning but I've always loved orange lilies."

"What does it mean?" I asked.

"Well, it can have different meanings but it's most commonly known for hatred and disdain. Hold on…"

She paused, turning around to grab a white paper with green lettering. I could see a stack of identical copies as she turned back to offer one to me.

"This is a list of flowers and their meanings."

She smiled brightly as I clasped my thumb down and took the paper from her extended hand. I studied the list for an amount of time that seemed to satisfy her before looking back up.

"Can I get you anything else, dear?"

I turned briefly to take in the many scents behind me before looking back at her with a grin.

"No, that's all."

The next thing I knew, I was walking through the cemetery. The sun was bright but many grey clouds loomed in the distance, as if to mimic my uneasy emotion. I leaned forward with the lily in my hand, placing it atop my father's grave.

"Jesus!"

My hand leaped up to my chest as I looked over to find Sean standing beside me.

"Just because you *can* move undetected doesn't always mean you should. Can't you at least pretend to make normal foot sounds?"

Sean bumped my shoulder. "What fun would that be?"

"Idiot," I said, shaking my head as I looked toward our father's gravestone for the first time.

"I remember how excited he was to be able to pass that on to you."

I looked up to find Sean's grin as his eyes fell upon my Morgan bracelet. I quickly looked down, raising my left wrist to my face, trying to ignore that sad fact that my dad never got the chance to give it to me. I could imagine him holding an internal excitement that would have been similar to when he decided to wrap my Jetta with a ridiculous big red bow.

"Do you think he was proud of us, or disappointed?" I asked, not looking away from the bracelet but not quite looking at it either.

"Why would he be disappointed..." Sean paused with a teasing smirk. "Other than for either of us not attending Duke."

I exhaled amusement at the thought as my eyes scanned the engraving of "Paul Morgan" on the headstone.

"He may have been stubborn and he had no patience for those who didn't follow his advice but he loved you very much, Ems." My eyes closed for a moment of composure as I listened to my brother's words. "Let your last memory of him be that he loved you."

I shifted my eyes to look at the headstone, nodding at the dark thoughts within my mind.

"You know, it's funny how you've always wanted me to live a normal life, away from immortals. But my normal could very well be having an aneurism at 43."

I turned to my brother with my brow raised, exhaling with a humorless chuckle.

"Normal could even be bleeding out from a car accident at 22...or getting cancer at 35."

"Okay, I get your point."

His voice was calm but his words felt tense, as if I had caught him off guard. I looked up to see his lips straight, anticipating my response.

"Do you, though?"

Sean remained quiet, turning his brightened honey gaze on me.

"You have to let go, Sean, and accept that you can't protect me from what's meant to happen."

"What am I supposed to do if I can't protect my little sister?"

The waver in his voice pained me.

"Though you always seem to take on the role of my protector, that was never your job, Sean."

I reached over, taking his hand in mine as I leaned into his shoulder.

"What is my role, then?"

It felt as if a slither of light had peeked through a dark tunnel of the impasse where we'd been stuck for so long.

"Just help me be happy for however long I have."

My temple lay against his shoulder but my eyes focused on the flower on my father's grave. An image of an identical headstone appeared within my mind, reading *Emma Rose Morgan, beloved daughter and sister.* Standing alone was Sean, holding a bouquet of lilies that he now placed at *my* grave.

Whether that be tomorrow or 70 years from now.

I didn't speak my last words aloud but he heard them nonetheless, just as he would have seen the image in my mind a few seconds ago.

My head rose to watch his jaw clench, attempting to shake the image from his thoughts. Quickly, I brought forward the memory of our reunion a year ago. I watched as the tension faded from his jaw, replaced with elation at the memory we shared.

"Can I ask you something?" I said.

"Sure."

"Would you have stayed gone?"

His mouth opened to speak but he seemed unable to find the right words. My heart raced with trepidation. When he finally spoke, it was not to me but to the grass that lay at our feet near the headstone.

"For the rest of your life, I would have never interfered again."

I took a breath as if readying myself, only to look down while I spoke.

"But would I interfere with yours?"

My last word came out in a stumble but I looked up with a burst of courage to see that he couldn't quite manage the same. It took a few seconds longer before his head finally rose, revealing the brightest golden hazel I had ever seen from him since discovering his secret immortality.

"Always."

He said nothing but I could read the pain of his expression as he let go of my hand. The very issue I had spoken about before had come back to face him head-on.

"Your anger on the surface focuses on Liam but from what you said about Grace, you were mostly just angry with yourself for interfering a year ago."

He looked off toward the distant headstones of the graveyard. I put my hand on his bicep, intending to pull his focus.

"Sherlock's got nothing on you," Sean teased.

"So why did you stay after you arranged for us to come back?"

"I ask myself that every day and yet I can come up with only one answer."

"What?"

His eyes rose to mine once again, gazing back at me as if the answer should be obvious.

"I couldn't leave you behind."

I exhaled at the contradiction between his reasoning and his reaction.

"I don't want you to be filled with self-deprecation for the rest of your immortal life."

"I know you don't but whether you want it to or not, it won't disappear just because you ask it to. Not in your lifetime, at least."

It felt as if the conversation wasn't over and yet this session had reached its limit. Sean looked at the silver designer watch on his wrist while mindlessly asking, "So…are you going to prom?"

I resisted a smirk over a familiar conversation with my friends that had started with that same question weeks ago…

…

"Nobody said yes," Matt Barnes said jokingly to the unlikeness of someone as popular and good-looking as Michael not having his pick of girls.

"Nah, I just didn't realize that it was on the same night as something I have to do for my dad."

I eyed him questioningly as he glanced at me for a second before turning back to the banter from the guys.

"Maybe he's just going to another school's prom," Ben said with laughter before Becca elbowed him in the stomach while looking over at me. I held her uncomfortable gaze for only a second, wishing Patrick had swiped the memory of Liam's ever leaving so that I could have avoided those types of stares.

"What about Michelle Evans or Natalie Reamer?"

"I know Natalie is eager for you to ask her at least," Pamela said.

Michael rolled his eyes but his body language told me he would inevitably give in to the peer pressure. But what he actually said was, "I'll think about it."

.....

I shook my head, coming out of my reverie once again as I heard Sean's chuckle. It was as if he were standing in the background of my memories every time I revisited them.

"Right," Sean said as if not needing to dive further into the question. "What do you say we head back, then?"

I began to turn but suddenly paused.

"Wait, can you give me a second?"

I looked up to see Sean turn and nod once with understanding before he was suddenly out of sight.

From there, I turned back to the headstone, kneeling to place my palm against the stone. I had refused to come here for many reasons but I realized the true explanation for why I avoided my father's grave was because I knew it was my future too. It may be soon or it may be decades from now but inevitably I would follow him into death.

I was human and I couldn't escape that. But my avoidance didn't come from my fear of death. It was having to leave the looming sadness that would carry on in the two I loved most. One day they would be standing here, looking down at a gravestone that had my name on it. One that would remind them both that I was forever gone while they had to remain. That was the hardest part to accept.

I took a deep breath and nodded before turning to meet Sean, who had been waiting for me ten stones over. I reached out and took his hand, watching as he looked down, a smile forming before he looked back at me.

I couldn't take that fear of losing me away from any of us, but I could at least give him purpose until that moment did come.

"I need you to know something. Something to tell Liam when I'm gone."

I let the image of the children in my mind play for Sean, letting him get the clear picture with full access.

"I don't know if he'll ever truly believe that what I say doesn't come with resentment, so I want him to know there wasn't any."

I sighed.

"I don't even know if I'd want them or not. All I know for certain is that I'd never want to bring a life into this world if it wasn't his and mine together."

Sean nodded but I knew by his stare that he wasn't fully complying quite yet.

"I'll tell him but on one condition," Sean said.

"What?"

"I'm going to ask you a question. And I'll repeat it every five years."

"Okay," I said cautiously.

"You must always answer truthfully each time. If, and only if, your answer remains the same, then I'll tell him. But if you change your mind at any point during your lifetime, I'll remain silent. Deal?"

He dropped our linked hands so that he could step back and allow himself to extend his arm. He stood, ready to shake on the pact he had created. I shook my head, rolling my eyes while a grin crept across my face.

"Deal," I said, lifting my hand to meet his own. "Now, ask away."

"Knowing Liam can never father a child, if you had the chance to have one of your own, would you take it?"

My neck pulled back to focus on my brother as if to convey the seriousness of his question. But my lips merely pulled up with comfort at my accepted choice.

"No."

CHAPTER 15

Rogue Warrior

I had barely walked through the door of the Alexander home when I found Lillian waiting for me with a large, toothy grin.

"We'll take it from here," Lillian said.

She reached forward to take my hand before leading me up the stairs. I looked over my shoulder to see my boyfriend's wink as he watched his sister briefly kidnap me.

Lillian led me into one of the rooms across the hall from Liam's. The room had been set up as their own salon for the day. Grace held the same beaming smile that Lillian carried as I walked through the opening. I moved without hesitation to the readied chair that Grace pulled out for me.

"Let's do this," I said.

Once my make-up was lightly applied and my hair was styled up, Grace held my royal blue A-line, strapless sweetheart bodice dress at an angle. Lillian swiftly moved to my side in order to guide me into the perfect position to step into the dress. I was certain that without help I would have fallen or ripped the material.

As soon as I was straight, Grace pulled the dress over my bra, then adjusted my locket on the outside before beginning to lace up the corset-style back. Lillian fluffed out the bottom of the ballroom gown while Grace moved to ready the full-length mirror. Once they both stood back, I turned toward the mirror, my head pulling back dramatically at the sight of myself. I chuckled as the two girls behind me high-fived each other.

I smiled as my hand rose to touch the gold locket, which had led Lillian to find the gold chain and royal blue beaded chandelier earrings that I was also wearing

"You guys do beautiful work. Thank you," I said.

I turned around and looked between my sister-in-law and Lillian, truly grateful to have them in my life.

"You know we love to do it," Lillian said.

"Now let's go find you a prince," Grace teased.

With their help, I walked down the stairs to see that my mother had arrived with my uncle. Mary had told me a few days ago that she called to invite them over so that my mom wouldn't miss out on getting to take pictures this year.

"You look so beautiful, Ems. Wait, let me get one of you."

It was adorable how excited she was. I made sure to stop and pose so that she could get her candid shot.

Of course, turning my head, I became distracted by the beautiful, angelic, immortal looking straight at me. Liam was studying me as if afraid that if he looked away, he might miss an important moment.

He walked closer, looking beyond stunning in his black tuxedo and royal blue vest and tie that matched my dress. He moved toward the end of the staircase, extending his arm in a way that made me believe we had been thrown into a 19th-century novel.

My cheeks filled with warmth and my eyes moved back and forth with his own as I took his arm in mine with a wide smile. I could hear Mary ask my mom if she wanted a shot of Liam and me together.

"Oh no, the way they're looking at each other is way better than any posed shot."

I turned to them with a small blush before Liam lightly squeezed my arm. "Ready?"

"I am," I said, trying my best to resist the strong urge to kiss him. Everyone said goodbye as we made our way out the door. I looked up from the porch to see Sean standing across the way, near one of the trees. He blew me a kiss, which I pretended to catch and latch to my heart before Liam guided me down the steps and toward the silver Mercedes-Benz SLR McLaren waiting for us on the curved driveway.

Once we arrived at prom, Liam parked as close to the curb as possible. Without a moment for reflection, he stood outside my open butterfly-style door. He extended his hand, using the other to guide me out of the car with Hollywood grace.

As I stood on the curb, a slow curtain smile emerged as he curled an index finger to hold my chin and leaned in to gently kiss my lips. It seemed I wasn't the only one unable to resist the urge.

"I'll be right back," he whispered into my ear as he let go of our lips' embrace.

The ecstasy lingered through his fingertips as he lifted his hand from my cheek.

"Okay," I said while gesturing over to the left, where a stone bench was protruding from a group of trees. "I'll be over there by that bench."

He nodded but his gaze focused on my features for a long second before he finally moved swiftly to the running engine of his Mercedes. As he drove off, I walked down the sidewalk, away from the entrance and toward the group of slanted trees and the stone bench.

I waved at Erika and Mark as they entered the lit-up stair entrance. She wore a long, coral strapless dress and her hair was halfway up with long, wavy curls.

She mouthed the words, *See you inside,* while she pointed toward the building. I could see Mark enviously eyeing the Mercedes that had just driven off but once he felt the movement from Erika's arm, he quickly followed his date up the stairs.

Straight across the way, I caught sight of Michael, who must have seen me at the same time. I waved just as I caught sight of his date, Natalie Reamer, who was wearing a powder blue dress draped with a white shawl. I couldn't help but smirk as he rolled his eyes once she pulled on his arm for attention.

I'll pay for that later, I thought.

I started making my way toward the bench before changing my mind as I caught sight of the sycamore trees.

"Emma."

At the whisper-like call, I turned my neck. Suddenly, a prickle of hair rose on my neck and arms. My head looked left to right in a suspicious way before I turned my body in a full 360 circle. Maybe it was all in my mind. That was the easiest thing to rationalize, right?

"Emma…"

With the second call of my name, I looked back over my shoulder. My eyes searched around the brick building but were met with nothing.

"Emma…"

I rolled my eyes before turning around completely to face the empty space.

"Liam, where are you—"

I turned back toward the bench but with all the time I'd spent looking behind me, I hadn't considered who might appear in front of me. My hand flew to my stomach in an odd form of protection as I took in the stranger. He stood no taller than Michael, with dirty blond hair and bright brown eyes that were a slightly darker shade than Lillian's. His head was tilted and his mouth twisted into a cruel smile that I felt I'd come to know all too well.

"Thomas sent you," I said.

It wasn't a question but a statement of verification. Oddly, the man remained silent. Even *I* knew the thrill for Thomas came from his need to taunt his prey. The same would be for any of his minions, like Ben and Fiona on the boat. This was out of character and I had to admit it held me on a borderline of confusion.

I opened my mouth to awaken his silence but the force of his right hand flung to my neck, leaving me speechless. My eyes widened in terror as the pleasure of my painful capture seeped into his sadistic bloodstream.

I didn't have to be a doctor to know that a bruise was forming from his crushing grasp. But the thought of my throat was quickly forgotten as I was thrown backward by his strength with a speed and precession that left me defenseless. There wasn't even time to mentally brace myself before my body collided with the brick wall, pushing my chest unnaturally forward as I slumped to the grass.

My lungs were helplessly choking, refusing to allow in any oxygen as the warm, moist liquid on the back of my head begin to move closer to my temple. I tried to prevent my mind from shutting down but I knew inevitably the pull would be too strong to resist. For once, I just closed my eyes and welcomed the black void like an old friend.

CHAPTER 16

Expected and Unprepared

It was similar to those moments when you convince yourself that you'll close your eyes for only a few seconds and then, suddenly, you're lured into the blissful sensation of sleep. I wasn't sure how much time had passed but I knew, when I opened my eyes again, that I was within the safe cradle of Liam's arms.

His sculpted cheekbones held an edge that I wished to dissolve but my eyelids were manipulated once again into blackness. It was as if my mind could handle consciousness for only minutes at a time before needing to reset. I awoke again to realize I had been placed upright in the front seat of Liam's car.

"Emma, love…can you hear me?"

My chest felt as if a brick were pressing down onto it but somehow I found the strength to move my hand to the side of my head. The familiar warm and moist liquid slowly crept farther down my face. As I pulled back my hand, I saw the dark red glisten over my entire palm.

"What happened?"

Despite the short sentence, the words came out in a strained breath. I attempted to turn with instant regret as pain suddenly released, as if on command, in opposite directions of my body, forcing me to grunt loudly as if the sound were a way to seek relief.

"Don't try to move," Liam said.

I wasn't sure how it was possible to find a combination of fury and pure terror in someone's gaze and yet the balance danced perfectly in Liam's bright green eyes.

I lay my head to rest on the seat, desperate to keep him within view but knowing the clock was ticking on my consciousness. I could feel the growing monster of pain taunting me for its own pleasure. I was ready to slump over in defeat if it would make the pain stop.

"I should never have left you," Liam said.

I wanted to place my hand on his face with reassurance, but I couldn't force my arms to move. It was as if invisible sandbags were weighing them down. I opened my mouth to speak the only words that took no effort.

"I love you."

I could feel my small lifted grin as the ghosts of the void began to pull me back under—but not before cruelly taunting me with the fading memory of Liam reaching over to cup my face and whisper, "Emma, stay with me."

The air circled my face as Liam moved, unblocked, into the mansion. My head tipped back, my eyelids too heavy to reopen, forcing me to blindly listen to the echoed chaos around me.

"She's been in and out of consciousness," Liam stated.

"Place her there."

Mary held a calm and concentrated voice that one would expect from an experienced ER doctor. I felt the slow, delicate placement of the cushioned hospital bed but Liam's touch lingered underneath my back as if he was terrified to let go. It was enough motivation to fight the closed curtain of my eyelids, at least if only for a little while.

Grace was buzzing around the room with her immortal speed, allowing me to see her outline only when she stopped at each station with supplies.

"Everything…Everything hurts."

Mary placed a hand upon my cheek as if desperate for me to focus all the pain back onto her beautiful blue eyes. My gaze shifted around slightly to note that she was dressed in blue surgical scrubs. Her hair was tied back and covered in a light blue surgical cap.

"I know, sweet girl," Mary said.

My vision was becoming blurred by the warm tears that fell unevenly out of the corner of my eyes. I felt the cold touch of her fingertips on my scalp, which always occurred when she was using her healing gift.

"You've been so brave but I need you to stay with me a little longer, okay?"

Though we both knew different. I nodded in compliance before my eyes closed involuntarily. I felt the sharp needle prick into my right arm with the simultaneous hard rip of my entire dress as it was torn away from my body.

"She's lost too much blood," Mary stated with a disappointed urgency. "Liam give me…"

"A negative, here."

Liam's voice sounded as if he was standing above my head. That meant he must have been hooking up the pint of blood that would be transferred into the IV attached to my arm. My senses were going as the overpowered lure was beginning to pull me back down into unconsciousness. I knew couldn't hold on much longer.

"Mary, her vitals are dropping."

"She's going into cardiac arrest," Mary shouted.

Without warning, the ghosts pulled me into the void but it wasn't the familiar one that I usually had no memory of while unconscious. Terrifyingly, I found myself blindly trapped within my own mind, forced to listen to the echo of my death. It was as if someone else was live-projecting their memory into my mind.

"Charge to 300," Mary commanded.

"Charged to 300," Grace said.

It was subtle but I could hear the flat line as Mary must have quickly rubbed the defibrillator pads in a circular motion.

"Clear!"

147

Suddenly, I felt an upward pull as I was thrown back into the cold, dark void like a rag doll.

Emma.

Unlike the familiar unconscious void, this new place in my mind was focusing on the call of a singular voice. It called to me as if I were a terrified child looking for my mother.

I need you to fight, Emma.

Who was reaching for me in this cold, dark abyss?

Don't you dare leave. Fight, Emma.

The voice grew louder, becoming more distinct. If I had a little more time, I could figure out who it was and how to get to them.

FIGHT!

CHAPTER 17

Impolite Request

Slowly, my mind lifted from the dense fog of unconsciousness but my eyes took longer to convince. I blinked several times into a squinted gaze but was unable to avoid the small stabbing pain caused by the bright light directly hitting my pupils.

If I wasn't aware of the nightmare that I had just come through, the IV pumping fluid into my body was a harsh reminder. Even worse were the delayed flashes of my memory that had cruelly waited until my mind was alert before they began to fly at me like a flock of savage birds.

The strange behavior behind the bright, unfamiliar immortal gaze. The painful gasping for air as my lungs refused to let me breathe. The warm liquid of my blood imprinted onto my hand. The beckoning voice that encouraged me to battle through the instinct to let go.

I squeezed my eyes shut like a child believing the monster in the dark would disappear if she merely pulled the covers over her head. I exhaled, focusing on the beeping in my ear, which I knew without looking was the heart rate monitor attached to my left index finger.

"This is becoming a tradition I'm not fond of."

My eyes immediately opened again to the calming sound that alerted my nerves like a mental Xanax. My gaze started on the dirty blond waves of his hair, then circled the outline of his jaw before making its way up to the bright emerald green eyes I loved so much.

"That makes two of us," I said.

He reached down to cup my face with a gentle grasp as if imprinting it through his fingertips. My eyes shifted to the closed hardback book in his hands.

"Don't you think that's a little on the nose?" I teased while tilting my head toward his blue-colored copy of Jane Austen's *Emma*.

"This is just a coincidence," Liam bantered back as he leaned down to kiss my forehead.

"How long has it been this time?"

It was odd how normal that question was starting to become.

"Mary wanted to access any further complications so she has kept you in an induced coma for a week."

"That bad, huh?"

I reached up to lay my hand against the tension in Liam's jaw but the way he slowly smoothed my wrist with his thumb told me my attempt at humor wasn't enough. I remained silent as he moved to sit back down, holding a tight grin. He may not have shown his emotions as easily as my brother did but that didn't mean dealing with the attacks on my life was easy on him.

"I really thought I was going to lose you."

He paused, as if more thoughts were surfacing but he refused to let the words loose to me.

"Not yet," I said.

Liam froze, straightening his body as if he were an animal in the woods that had become alert to a threat.

"What's wrong?"

He stood without answering. My eyes followed his reach as he grabbed my phone from the nightstand.

"Michael has been calling."

I narrowed my eyes at the subject change, envious of his immortal hearing at that moment.

"I'll give you some privacy to reassure your friend while I go check in with Patrick."

"There's something you're not telling me," I said. I looked around his face, searching for a crack in his defense that might let me in. "But you're right, I should call Michael back."

Liam merely nodded in compromise before disappearing out of sight. I sighed in frustration before looking down to see 20 missed calls and 35 unread text messages. So much for him not noticing I hadn't walked into prom. By the time I'd found the energy to lift the phone to my ear, Michael's worried voice was already coming through the receiver.

"Emma?"

By the way he said my name, it was as if he was prepared to hear someone else alerting him to bad news.

"Yeah, it's me."

"Are you ok?"

"I'm fine. What's with all the missed calls?"

My mind could practically see his blue eyes narrowing with incredulous disbelief at such a question. I had to admit that if the roles were reversed, I would have shown the same worry. It wasn't exactly normal to suddenly disappear from prom and then not show at school all week.

"Uh…"

The waver in his voice came from the new leak of doubt caused by my nonchalance. His confusion had most likely thrown him into believing that his worry had come across as exaggerated. "I just noticed you never made it into prom…it was like you disappeared or something after I saw you outside." There was a long pause, as if he was finding it difficult to get through the awkwardness of the moment. "I thought you might have gotten sick or something. Especially since you haven't been at school either."

"I was feeling kind of odd while getting ready for prom but thought it would go away by the time we got there."

"I'm guessing since you left, it didn't get better?"

"No. By the time Liam walked up to find me, we both knew I needed to head home."

"Well, it's been like a week without you in school so…"

I knew the pause in his sentence was Michael's way of fishing for an answer. I mentally prepared myself before jumping into my false pretense.

"Yeah, it turns out it was the early signs of the flu. That's why I've been out of school all week. I would have called you sooner but this is the first day I've had the energy."

"Oh, don't worry about it. I should have thought to call your mom or uncle. Even Erika mentioned she thought you were probably sick but I was just worried when I hadn't heard from you." Finally, it was his turn to sigh. "Ugh, this all sounds dumb now but maybe I was still feeling guilty about giving you the cold shoulder for so long."

"Well, did *you* at least have a good time at prom?"

"Um…kinda." It was my turn to be suspicious. "I wasn't really feeling it so we left a little early."

"Oh, Michael."

"I know, but to be fair I didn't think my date was going to talk about 'Grey's Anatomy' the whole dance." He sighed while I tried to resist laughing. "I honestly should never have admitted that I've never seen the show."

"Yikes," I said. "Well, hopefully, she's not a big fan of that show 'Revenge.'"

"That makes two of us," Michael said.

I giggled just as I looked up to see Liam's smile in the doorway.

"Well, I'd better go. I'm just now having the energy to shower and I really need one."

"Oh yeah, go ahead. I'll see you at school on Monday?"

"The doctor cleared me," I said, looking at Liam as he sat on my bed with a smirk he was clearly trying to resist. "So I'll be there."

"Alright. Take it easy until then," Michael said.

"Bye, *Mom*."

"Bye, loser."

"I hear the flu has been pretty bad this year," Liam said as I hung up.

I rolled my eyes before looking back at him with a mischievous grin.

"We're just lucky you didn't come down with it too."

"I've been blessed with an impeccable human immune system," Liam said with a teasing shrug.

"Yeah. Speaking of that impeccable immune system, do you think it could help me to the shower?"

Liam reached out his hand. "Your wish is my command."

The next day, I took advantage of the blissful state that came from resting my full body back against Liam's on the living room couch. Both of us were lost within the fantasy of a novel as he mindlessly ran his free hand through my hair.

The blissful peace was suddenly interrupted when the side window, near the front of the Alexander home, shattered. I dropped my book as Liam moved swiftly to lift us from the couch. By the time my mind caught up, he had set us down near the foot of the stairs as his body protectively stood in front of mine.

My hands grasped his shirt as I peeked around at the glass spread on the ground in all directions. It dawned on me that Liam had moved us to an area where my bare feet were protected.

Though Liam still held out his arm, I moved around him enough to see what had caused the destruction. It was a body. An immortal body. And despite me not knowing the stranger personally, I recognized him in an instant. It was the immortal who had ruined my prom and came close to taking my life a week ago.

But there was a clear difference between the immortal that confronted me and the one currently lying motionless on the Alexander Mansion floor. The thickened veins and grey-colored skin made it clear that he had met the same fate he had intended for me.

My stomach clenched as I looked around the room to find every single Alexander, including my brother, surrounding the dead immortal.

I heard the sound of glass cracking under the weight of shoes as Sean—who stood closest to the body—walked the short distance. He kneeled down, all eyes watching as he grabbed the white paper that had been pinned to the dead immortal's blue cotton shirt.

Sean stood, his eyes meeting mine before looking back down at the note. I seemed to have an excess of saliva, forcing me to gulp several times as he began reading the impolite request.

Alexanders,

Despite young Liam's treachery, I have come to a fair compromise that will leave your coven intact. Give me Emma Morgan by week's end and you will receive no further consequences. Decline my request by keeping her hidden and I will make sure you all meet the same fate as Fredrick here.

I recommend you choose wisely so that you don't force the girl to helplessly watch as I eliminate the Alexander Coven, one by one, from her life.

Your clock starts now.

-Thomas

CHAPTER 18

Beta Order

The silence of the room sent an eerie chill down my spine. I looked over to meet Sean's bright gaze and tense jawline, readying myself for the fight about to leave his mouth. At least that was until a knock at the door alerted every immortal in the room.

Within seconds, Liam moved his arm back as he stepped squarely in front of me. I felt a cool sensation radiating from my back but I didn't need to turn my neck to know that Lillian had protectively jumped into an invisible shield behind me.

"It's Charlie," William said.

Everyone turned their eyes on Sean. His shoulders remained on guard but his head tilted back toward Patrick with confused caution. He was reading Charlie but I knew from his furrowed brow that he wasn't sure whether to trust the thoughts from the other side of the door. But I also knew which had won out, as Sean simply nodded in communication to the room.

The cold of Lillian's invisibility faded as she walked to the center of the room. I gazed back at Sean, who had been waiting for my attention. He silently signaled me with his index finger on his lips before tapping his nose twice. It was something he had developed when we were kids. It meant, *No questions. Go along with it.*

Just as he did when I was little, Sean waited for me to nod back in compliance. Then he looked over at Patrick with approval to proceed. I slid my hand inside Liam's as Patrick opened the door with a smile.

"Charlie, good to see you. Come in."

"Likewise, Patrick."

As he stepped through the doorway and into the Alexander Mansion, Charlie's smile was genuine, just as I remembered it from Sean's wedding.

"What brings you by?"

"I've been looking for my sister and I've heard rumors about her in your territory," Charlie said.

"We've had a few encounters from her associates but nothing direct," Patrick confirmed.

Slowly, Charlie turned his neck, nodding his understanding of Patrick's words as he stared at me.

"It appears she has followed in Henry's footsteps." Charlie paused to bounce his gaze over at Liam, his shoulders dropping with disappointment. "But I guess you would have already known that."

"Yes," Liam said.

My boyfriend's words were neither gentle nor polite.

"I'm sorry for intruding," Charlie said while looking at Liam's and my linked hands.

"We're always happy to see you, Charlie," Mary said.

"Your kindness precedes you, as always," Charlie said with a gaze appearing to be lost within the memories he once shared with his former Roamer Coven.

"What brings you to us?"

There was a more business-like tone within Patrick's words, unlike the pleasantness he had shown moments before.

"I'm not the only one who has seen my sister's disloyalty." I could hear the pain in his voice, as if Jane's actions had weighed him down with a heavy heart. If I had any doubt about whether he was aware of Jane's plan, his next words confirmed it.

"Marius has executed the Beta Order."

"Beta Order?"

There were moments like this when I—and every immortal in the room—were reminded of how human I really was. All eyes turned toward me, including Charlie's, but it was Liam who spoke to me with his tender, soft voice.

"When the New Order was established, Marius initiated a Beta Oath to be recited by each immortal after their transformation. It was to ensure we committed to carrying out a Beta Order if Marius gave one."

By the insinuation of his words, I already knew what that *commitment* meant, and yet I still needed to hear it out loud before I would believe it.

"When does he *give* the Beta Order?"

"Once an immortal takes the life of a human, it is the coven's responsibility—each member—to turn them back to the New Order. But if we fail…"

Charlie paused, his eyes full of bright regret as he moved with a cautious step forward. "Marius will execute the Beta Order for the remaining coven members to eliminate their immortal family member."

His gaze looked away from mine for just a moment, as if he were desperate to shift his emotions like his shapeshifting abilities. But as I studied his avoidance, something clicked within my mind.

"Was that why Jane was so furious about Henry's death?"

Charlie looked over at Patrick briefly before turning back to me, as if trying to determine the best way to avoid frightening me with his words.

"Yes." His hands rose toward his chin in pleading surrender. "But not in the way you might think. See, we both knew there was no returning Henry to his former soul. That anger from Jane came from a sense of failed duty."

Knowing what I did of Jane, that made another puzzle piece snap into the center. She was a bitch but there was no doubt that her immortal DNA had a code. Of course, she would feel as if she had failed the New Order upon learning that another coven had carried out the duty of taking out Henry.

It made even more sense that, in her immortal eyes, this undercover plan would have felt like a road to redemption. There was just one problem. The Beta Order had moved like a spotlight to find her on center stage, threatening the plan already in motion.

"A duty she inevitably gave up when she aligned herself with Thomas," Charlie said, his voice drawing me away from my worried thoughts. "Marius had no option but to execute the order in order to avoid history repeating itself."

My mind flashed to the memories of Liam's stories about his immortal kind. A vivid tale that always left me with a chill was that of Livius and Amara—an immortal Bonnie and Clyde who desired chaos over order.

And though the two had been killed before their plans could surface, their last loyal follower—Thomas—remained a chameleon to this day. It would make sense that the leader of all immortals couldn't risk Thomas pairing off with another and rekindling more chaos just as his immortal predecessor had done before him.

"So, you mean…"

"Yes," Charlie said with a nod. "I've been ordered to kill my sister."

I looked over at Sean only to see the same finger taps to his nose. *We have to tell him about what we're doing with Jane.*

Sean kept his eyes from mine. *Sean?* I could hear the irritation in my thoughts and was ready to protest until I finally caught my brother's eye.

There was a silent plea for me to resist, to remain quiet and trust him. It was then that I also felt Liam's hand squeeze mine, as if he knew about the silent battle between Sean and me. My eyes lifted to Liam's to find the same hopeful plea.

It was enough for me to relent as I watched Patrick step forward with his hand out.

"You'll let us know if you need anything?"

"Yes."

"Good luck," Patrick said.

Charlie reached out with his own hand, shook with the Alexander leader, and nodded in appreciation.

"Farwell, Alexanders. May we meet again."

He looked around at each immortal before focusing on me. Charlie smiled but said nothing. He held my gaze for only a few seconds before he was gone completely.

I stared at the door, contemplating my confusion by trying to seek Jane's guidance—as odd as that sounded—before looking up at Sean's waiting gaze.

As I reflected silently on the pleas from Liam and Sean, I realized that no one in the room felt good about lying to Charlie. But if Jane's plan was going to work without Thomas's suspicions, her own brother would have to believe her betrayal.

Sean's controlled nod was the confirmation I expected, which meant that the risk Jane had asked of me was also unknowingly extended to her brother. The only difference was that one of us was aware and the other was ignorant. And to be honest, I wasn't sure who had the worse deal.

CHAPTER 19

Finding Moments

When I woke the next morning, I tried to remember what normal felt like. The kind of normal that involved getting to enjoy prom without nearly dying. The kind of normal that involved cuddling with your boyfriend on the couch without a body flying through the window. But I guess *that* type of normal belonged to another lifetime.

As I walked down the hallway, I heard the normal chatter from my classmates. Some talked of whom they hooked up with after prom, others raved about the movie they saw on Sunday, and a few girls even stared in envy as my blond-haired immortal boyfriend leaned against my locker with a smile.

Not one had a clue of the real torment swarming my brain or knew about the threat looming so close to their town border. And I couldn't help but envy them for that, as I accepted that my normal would never be the same as theirs.

At lunch, Michael sat down with his eyes burning into my skin. It was as if he was trying to examine me for any sign of an illness that had reappeared.

"I'm fine," I said.

Michael nodded but his cautious stare made it obvious that he didn't quite believe my words.

"I'm fine, *Mom.*"

He rolled his eyes at my tease before turning back to the table's conversation. I squeezed Liam's hand in comforting ease. Unlike the false pretense I had made up for Michael, Liam's concern held merit. And though he may not have persisted in questioning me like Michael did, his glances were of the same nature.

I smiled up at him before looking toward the eyes I could feel on me from across the room. Natalie Reamer sat with her friends, glaring toward me with resentment and envy. It was clear that, despite her immaturity, she had figured out that Michael had feelings for someone else. If only she knew I was *never* going to be a threat.

And yet despite my polite smile, she narrowed her eyes at me with slight intimidation. *Enough of this.* I leaned toward Michael but spoke with a stage whisper, "Tell your girlfriend over there to quit giving me the evil eye."

I smirked at the desired effect of getting my friends to turn their eyes and stare at Natalie. It was enough intimidation for the junior girl to look away and strike up a conversation with her own table again.

"Nicely played," Liam said next to my ear before placing his lips to my temple.

I closed my eyes for a moment, letting myself get lost in the affection. I reached down to cup my locket, as if it helped harness the warmth that Liam's presence created. It was a moment to forget about jealous high school girls as much as it was to forget about Thomas's request.

I was almost irritated to be pulled from it when I heard Pamela's voice, popping the bubble with a question I didn't quite catch.

"What?"

She didn't hide the smirk that she shared with Becca as she leaned forward to ask again.

"I said, how many invitations did you send out?"

I saw Pamela's eyes looking at me inquisitively as her voice told me she had already asked everyone around the table. "Um…" I hadn't exactly paid attention to whether my mom had sent out invitations. I wasn't even sure what they looked like. Or if that was something I was supposed to order for her to send out. These were all details that seemed insignificant, as I wasn't even sure I was going to make it to graduation day.

"I think it was close to 30," I said, biting my lip and looking off to the side as if I were trying to remember.

"Is Sean going to be there?"

My eyes shifted slightly toward Erika, which caused Matt to turn his head with an unnecessary jealous worry. I found it hard to resist my gaze upon her neck, as if expecting to find the same exposed flesh and blood from the night on the boat. I looked down briefly, blinking excessively in the hopes that this would help me lose the awful memory, for a few minutes at least.

"Of course," I said, looking back up with a sincere smile. Or so I hoped it looked sincere.

Erika smiled back and patted the top of Matt's hand, which seemed to be slightly crushing the burger in his fingers.

"I just wanted to talk to him about campus living. I've decided to attend UNC. Did I tell you?"

"No, you didn't. That's great."

She nodded, eyeing the tense Matt, who had just relaxed at the platonic agenda of seeing Sean.

"Have you decided yet?"

It felt oddly morbid but when the moment came to my mind, I thought back to the nightmare that had caused my panic attack in Liam's room. Inspiration struck through my terror.

"I actually just received my acceptance letter from Stanford yesterday."

As I heard the praise from my friends, I turned to wink at Liam, who held his own prideful amusement.

"Where are *you* going?"

Michael sat with his body sideways, his head positioned around me to gaze at Liam.

"I haven't decided yet." I looked back at Liam, seeing his smile on me, which told me that Michael's on-the-spot question hadn't affected him. By the sound of his voice, I knew he had probably been prepared for weeks with that answer.

Michael opened his mouth, ready to ask more questions about the colleges that Liam had applied to, so I turned to the table quickly. "Where is everyone else going?"

Thankfully, it worked. By the end, I had learned that Erika was going to UNC, Lauren had received an unexpected acceptance to Virginia Tech, Pamela and Becca were rooming together next fall at East Carolina, and Heather had accepted a volleyball scholarship to Duke.

The latter held the least interest until my memory once again got lost in the events of that night on the boat. She may not have remembered her heroics but I certainly did.

"Congratulations, Heather," I said with a small smile.

"Thanks," Heather said as she narrowed her eyes before looking around at the others, who seemed just as surprised to hear my praise. I merely shrugged before looking down to finish my lunch.

Later that day, as Liam and I walked through my front door, I turned to look at him with inquisitiveness. He seemed to be resisting amusement over something.

"What?"

"Well, I decided to create a false pretense for you to use when it came to your mother. Funny thing is…"

He paused while reaching for something from his front pocket. Once he held it out, I could see that it was a white envelope with the Stanford seal in the top right corner.

"I also used your dream as inspiration."

"How very morbidly in sync we are," I said while reaching for one of my mom's letter openers. I sliced open the envelope and slid out the folded papers inside, then read the first page.

Dear Ms. Morgan,

Congratulations! It is with great pleasure that I offer you admission to the Stanford University class of 2014.

"Not that it matters but I'm surprised that I got in. Did you pay to put in a new library or something?"

"That was all on your own merits," Liam said if it were the most obvious thing in the world. "Now you have something if we—god willing—make it out of this plan alive."

"Like you said, let's just worry about Thomas first before you go trying to ship me across the country for my studies."

"Fair enough, but I do hear the weather's nice in California," Liam said while placing a stray hair behind my ear. His touch lingered down to my jawline.

"I hear the same thing about North Carolina," I bantered back with a grin before placing my finger in the air. "Wait, doesn't Stanford require an essay?"

His lips held a resisted smile full of guilt.

"I used the last one you wrote for English."

"Clever," I said as my eyes met the clock to my left.

My shoulders automatically dropped, as I knew it was time for Liam's Watch. With a sigh, I turned my full gaze back to him as he took in my anguish upon watching him leave. Reluctantly, I walked toward the front door with him before he turned to gently kiss me on the lips with restraint, knowing he wouldn't be able to let go if he lingered.

"I'll be back to hold you in my arms before you even have time to think about missing me."

"I doubt that," I said with a grin that matched his own.

We leaned our foreheads together, then lifted our gazes so that we met each other's eyes. Finally, I found the strength to let go, watching him open the door and disappear with a speed faster than my eyes were able to see.

I pushed air out of my lips as I looked back at the table. I glanced at the letter as I heard the garage door open. I looked back at the clock, confirming that my mom was right on time getting home. Instinctively, I reached for the letter. I knew, even if it may be a mere pretense, that it was important to take the moment for what it was: a daughter telling her mother that she had been accepted to college.

My life with the Alexanders wasn't about trying to get back to normal anymore. It was about finding moments between the terrifying shadows in the distance.

CHAPTER 20

Dream Invasion

I sat on the porch swing at the Alexander Mansion, listening to the warm breeze rustling the leaves against one another. My jean shorts and white t-shirt reminded me how odd it felt to know how much time had passed since I agreed to Jane's plan. One moment I was anxiously staring out my windshield in mid-winter and suddenly we were heading into the last legs of spring.

I sat in silence, my mind debating whether that was a good thing. Then, laughter coming out of the trees drew me away from my thoughts. But it wasn't the interruption of the sound that led to my new confusion. It was what I saw emerging from the tree line.

I quickly stood, watching as two young siblings stepped into view. Their laughter was contagious as they ran along the curved driveway, not caring about the sounds that bounced off the annoyance of the trees. My eyes studied the little boy, who was no older than five. He was an exact replica of Sean, who protectively held the hand of a younger version of me. I watched as the young boy encouraged his sister to play with the few fallen leaves at her feet.

Slowly, I began to move toward the porch steps, desperate to interact with them, until a strong hand on my shoulder stopped me. I turned to find Liam sternly gazing at me with his bright emerald eyes, causing my old world to collide with my new.

His free hand was curled into a fist and his jawline was unusually tense. My brow furrowed as he shook his head apologetically, finally releasing a familiar softness.

"You can't," Liam said.

"Why not?"

"It is forbidden after the order has been given."

I stepped back, my confusion growing.

"Order...what order?"

Suddenly, Patrick and Mary came to stand beside him, staring back at me as if they were the guards preventing me from entering the bank vault. My mouth began to dry, terror flowing through me with a heaviness that was too much to bear.

"I don't understand," I said, looking between the three immortals.

"There's no way out of the Beta Order," Mary said.

My neck turned back to see that the children were gone.

"No," I said. "He hasn't done anything. He'd *never* harm a human."

"He has," Patrick spoke. "And it's your responsibility to carry out the order."

"You can't make me do that." I shook my head vehemently. "He's my brother."

"You don't have a choice," Liam said regretfully. "It must be done."

I looked over my shoulder, gulping down the reality.

"Please," I begged.

The immortals remained silent, stepping aside to reveal Lillian and William, who were escorting Sean. Grace appeared from behind me, using one hand to cup the side of my face while the other placed something within my hand.

I looked down to see the foot-long steel piece in my right hand. It wasn't until Sean's knees hit the porch that I was able to bring myself to look up.

My brother's head hung low as William held his body down with his hands on his shoulders. My hands shook as each Alexander spoke with demanding encouragement to carry through with Sean's execution.

"You've taken the Oath."

"But I haven't. I'm not even an immortal," I said.

Even as the words left my lips, I knew they were useless.

"Human or immortal, you're part of this coven," Patrick said.

I could taste the salt of my tears, even though it was as if the shock had made me unaware of when they were released. Liam's soft lips were near the back of my ear.

"It's time."

His hand moved to mine, almost as if guiding me to move forward.

"I can't do this," I whispered.

My eyes locked on Sean's, watching his smile, the one I had known all my life. The one that reminded me of why he would always protect me.

"It's okay, Em," Sean said while nodding with finality. "It's okay."

And with his odd blessing, my hand pulled back as if I were pulling the string of wind-up toy. I silently counted to three before I lunged forward. One hand grasped his shoulder as the other punctured my brother's immortal heart, taking his life.

My eyes suddenly opened but my body remained horizontal as my chest rose sporadically with short breaths. I lay in silence as my mind realized I had been pulled out of another dream and thrown back into the reality of my dark bedroom.

I felt a chill run down my arms, the hairs pricking with the alert of an uninvited disturbance that I couldn't remember. I sat up expectantly and yet saw nothing in the darkness. My eyes adjusted to the night as I quickly turned and reached for the lamp on my right. But even with the new light, my confusion was only heightened when I felt a small breeze flowing through my room.

I looked toward my window, finding the open frame that I had remembered closing after Liam started his Watch.

Instinctively, I threw my comforter off my legs and walked over to the open window. My hands were still gripping near the locks when I looked up at the distant moon. My heartbeats had yet to slow as I turned back to my room, taking small steps back toward my bed. My eyes shifted around to every corner until I was trapped back within the safety of my sheets. I pulled my knees to my chest as my eyes continued scoping out the room.

When my focus landed back on the light nearest me, I was drawn down to my nightstand, where my lamp had illuminated a spotlight on a note. It seemed the writer had used the lamp as a paperweight, to prevent the note from floating away in the breeze. I had to hold the lamp base securely before I pulled the notebook paper from under it.

You are a divine creature when you slumber, even when trapped within nightmares.

-Thomas

My neck twitched involuntarily at the chill spreading down my arms. Thomas knew I had been having a nightmare because he had been in my room without the slightest difficulty of resistance. The chill had spread into several panicked shivers, my breath growing heavy with the realization.

The panic within my mind was stuck on fast forward. Was he still in my room or was he trying to scare me? He was an immortal, after all, and I knew how easily he could hide. I had seen Liam do it many times, anytime my mom walked into my room.

The window was closed and yet I still shivered with the note in my hand. I sat on my bed and pulled at the chain around my neck to adjust my locket as I waited for Liam. I knew he would be minutes away after Sean's telepathic news. If not Sean himself.

I debated opening the window again but couldn't find the motivation to get up. It was as if my mind had glued my legs to the bed. Instead, I sat looking back at the note, realizing that the scariest thing was not the invasion within my room. It was the tenderness behind the words of someone who took sadistic pleasure from drawing out my death.

Thomas had become my immortal stalker with an obsession, and that made him truly terrifying.

CHAPTER 21

Carry On

It was like being below the surface of a swimming pool. I was aware of the voices but couldn't quite find the discipline to listen. The radio signal of my mind was still searching for a clear station.

What I could detect was the strong pair of arms holding me close. I pressed my head into Liam's chest as his cheek lay on top of my head. It was unclear which of us needed the contact more.

Thomas had made a threat and then made it quite clear for those doubting him that he was capable of carrying through with it. Like me, Liam remained silent, merely soaking up the realization that had come upon us only a few hours ago. It wasn't until now that my mind had begun to unwrap itself from the protection it had formed—a protection that had been jolted into action due to my fear.

"Why the hell did we let ourselves agree to this?"

I should have known who my mind would allow me to hear first. My brother, who had resisted from the beginning, was full of his predictable rage. But the rage sounded different to me—not that I knew it was internalized at himself.

"You know we all agreed to the risk. We had a chance to go back but—"

Lillian spoke, not out of disloyalty but out of factual observation, only to be interrupted.

"Screw this. We can still—"

"Stop," I said, interrupting my brother this time, just as he had interrupted Lillian seconds before.

My voice was soft and yet I knew everyone would hear me. I straightened my torso while keeping my hands strongly attached to Liam. Every head turned, eyes gazing at me, anticipating my words.

"Lillian's right."

My eyes landed on her with playful scorn as I watched her lips rise with satisfaction. She merely nodded, keeping her gaze away from Sean.

"You were terrified," Sean said. "I can still see it as clear as Grace can feel it within you."

The way he observed me as he spoke made it obvious that he was remembering the images of my nightmare, trying to decipher their meaning within my mind. Of course, that only made them loop within my brain more.

"I'm not disagreeing on that point because it *was* terrifying." I paused, needing a minute to shake off the other image of myself stabbing my brother in my dream. "Only an ignorant fool would lie and say they weren't affected by it. But when haven't I been terrified these past months?"

"Then—"

"That's the whole point of this risk," I interrupted. "It was the whole point of getting ambushed on my friend's boat or almost dying at my own prom. Every single one of those moments terrified me, Sean. But don't forget, it was my choice from the beginning. She didn't demand anything. She suggested and I volunteered. So I might be scared out of my mind every second but that doesn't mean I take it back."

"I think our emotions—mine included—are heightened because of the other note," Grace said.

Every time she orbited near him, it became clear how perfectly fitted Grace was to my brother. Every word spoken and every touch felt was meant only for him.

His head turned, bringing about a true smile for what had felt lost for a year. It carried over as Grace brought up her hand to hold the side of his face.

But the sweetness of their moment was interrupted by my lingering confusion. *Other note?*

"Do you mean the first note that Thomas or…"

My thoughts drifted by the distraction of realizing that not every Alexander was in the living room.

"Watch," Liam confirmed.

His lips were speaking into the side of my head as he adjusted his body to cradle mine with a vertical hold. My instinct reached down to grasp his arms around my stomach.

"I guess Sean isn't the only one who can read my mind," I joked despite the humorless atmosphere.

He chuckled while placing a small kiss on my hair.

"Yes, the first note from Thomas," Lillian said.

By the time I adjusted my shoulder, Lillian had moved to sit next to me. Her hand was extended, holding a small piece of white paper. I reached out but her thumb resisted letting go until I met her eyes. The glowing brown spoke warningly as the other hand rose with one finger to her lips. It was clear that whatever I was about to read was not meant to be spoken aloud. That meant my instinct was right and we *were* talking about a third note.

I nodded with understanding, despite feeling a slight twitch of nerves, as I grabbed the paper she now permitted me to take.

Let him have her.

I inhaled deeply as I looked up and around the room, my gaze landing on my brother. It clicked, from the secrecy of the note, why I had to sign a verbal contract of silence with Lillian.

"Who…"

"Ems," Sean said with urgency. My words paused as all immortal eyes on me looked unsure of whether I would cooperate with the silent agreement. I focused on my brother, sending my question without the need for words.

Jane sent this?

Sean nodded.

"Do we know if Thomas will stay true to his deadline?"

Every immortal knew of the meaning behind my question but it was Liam who spoke from behind me. I understood the tension of the room even better now that I had been let in on Jane's hidden note.

"Nothing is exact but—"

"So, we have to be prepared that it could be any day," I said.

"Yes," Liam confirmed.

My back straightened. I was quite aware that it could all have been over for me within seconds tonight if Thomas wanted. But if I had learned anything about him, it was the knowledge that an easily captured pawn was no fun. Instead, Thomas was merely boasting about how easily he *would* win no matter how hard we made the game for him.

It was enough to make me want to give up but I knew the game we were playing was about more players than me. So, despite the instinct to cower, I knew I had to let myself be baited. The point had never been about surviving anyway.

"In that case..." I sighed, looking up at Sean with an intensity like that of an out-of-body warrior—one that ignored the fear encircling Jane's request. Sean's head was still but the bounce of his eyes revealed that he understood my oncoming words.

"We carry on."

I looked at Liam, silently communicating despite his not having Sean's ability. I needed him to keep the promise he had made in his bedroom. *Don't let it be for nothing.* I waited until I saw him nod back with consent before I looked over at Sean's tense bright honey gaze. I repeated the mantra in my mind, waiting for him to convey the same promise. Though there was much reluctance, my brother inevitably nodded back with acceptance.

Whatever may come, we carry on. I said the words over and over as if they were a battle cry. *Whatever may come, we carry on.*

CHAPTER 22

Bad Luck

I reached into the fridge and grabbed a Sprite can just as the doorbell rang. My hand retreated without the soda before I turned to look over my shoulder with my lips pursed in confusion. My mom would have used the garage, Michael had mentioned he was visiting the Georgia campus this weekend, and Liam—who had an hour left on his Watch—always greeted me at my bedroom window.

Jane's note echoed in my mind as I walked cautiously into the living room. We had one day left before I was officially meant to be handed over to Thomas. One day before we were ordered by Jane to let him *have me* without knowing the plan that followed. Was this him politely requesting to kidnap me?

My fearful thoughts were interrupted by two knocks along with a familiar voice on the other side of the door.

"It's Lillian."

I breathed a sigh of relief as I made my way over to the door and swung it open.

"This is a surprise," I said.

"Fancy a joy ride?"

"Did we have plans that I don't know about?"

"Nope," Lillian said with a simple shake of her head.

"It's been a while since you've spontaneously come over like this," I said with narrowed eyes of suspicion.

"Does that mean you're in?" Lillian asked with a challenge in her raised brow.

"Um...ok," I said while shrugging.

Who knew how much longer I had, so why not enjoy a spontaneous ride with Liam's immortal sister?

"Excellent," Lillian said victoriously.

"Where's Grace?"

"We don't do everything together, you know," Lillian said in a deadpan voice as we made our way down the porch steps.

"I know," I said while opening the passenger side door of her Mustang. "It's just—"

Lillian cut me off with her laughter, exposing her teasing as she made her way into the driver's seat. "Someone had to occupy Sean for this mission."

"Oh jeez, what are we *actually* doing that he wouldn't approve of?"

"If I told you, then he'd know." Lillian winked at me. "Sorry, Seanny."

I couldn't resist my own satisfied grin at the way she openly teased Sean, knowing he would be unable to resist reading my mind from the moment Lillian showed up on my doorstep.

I nodded with approval as she started the engine of her silver sports car, whose top was down.

"Let's go."

An hour and a half later, I found Lillian's intentions finally revealed as I stood in front of a full-length mirror inside her home. My hair, make-up, and blue ball gown were identical to the prom style that she had mastered over a month ago.

"You're truly talented. Does this mean my surprise is—"

My words were interrupted by Sean coming through the door, with Grace on his heels.

"You didn't think that was actually going to work for long, did you?"

"I didn't need it to. Just long enough for this," Lillian said while gesturing toward me with her hands.

Their rivalry wasn't as intense as it had been before he went missing but every so often I could sense an underlying irritation on Lillian's side. However, instead of it being about her past, it had morphed into protection over me.

"Look how cute she looks," Grace said with perfectly distracted timing. She held Sean's arm affectionately while winking at Lillian.

"Not fair," Sean said while looking over at Grace.

Though she could have easily done so, she rarely used her gift on Sean. I had to admit, it was fun seeing the natural adoration my brother had for his wife.

"None of us knows exactly how this will play out, so let her have a piece of normal," Grace said.

Sean remained quiet as he leaned in to kiss his wife's forehead. As his gaze lifted to mine, I could tell he was contemplating the risk.

Just let me have this last bit of fun before everything goes to hell.

Sean rolled his eyes, which was a sign that he had backed off in defeat. Lillian and Grace had played this one well.

"Go have fun," Sean said.

"Thanks," I said with a tooth-revealing smile.

"Your date has arrived, my lady," Lillian said with her hands cupping each of my shoulders.

The knowledge that Liam was behind the door caused butterflies to chaotically fly around in my stomach. I followed Lillian's lead toward the front door, unable to keep my cheeks from lifting as Grace opened it.

Liam stood on the front porch, dressed in a tailored black suit identical to the one he'd worn a month ago. Suddenly, something else joined the butterflies. It was hard to push down the lust-filled hormones rushing through me as my immortal boyfriend smiled back at me.

"Shall we try this again?" Liam said while lifting the familiar wrist corsage.

"I don't see why not," I said.

He gently slid the white rose around my wrist before his gaze slowly lifted to meet my blush-filled cheeks.

"You look beautiful," Liam said.

"I feel like I've heard that before in a situation similar to this," I teased.

"That may be but it bears repeating."

"Let's just try not to make this one like the last prom, huh?"

At Sean's words, I turned my head back, noticing how much closer the other four had gotten to Liam and me on the porch.

"I'll do my best," I said.

"Get out of here, you brat," Sean said.

"Alright, we're going. Don't wait up, *Dad*."

I grabbed Liam's hand, hearing his much-needed laughter as he guided me down the few steps. His BMW was parked out front, ready for our departure.

"Are we going far?"

"Not too far," Liam said with a smirk as he started the engine.

A few minutes later, we pulled into the curved driveway of the Alexander Mansion. My door opened and Liam extended his hand to help me from the car. He waited for our fingers to entwine before leading me around the back of the mansion. My mouth hung open at the sight.

A wooden floor was centered under a perimeter of hanging lights that dropped down, with silver and black balloons woven between them. A large metal replica of the Eiffel Tower stood between two large tables draped in thick black and silver cloth.

187

One table was stacked with dripping champagne glasses while the other held a large chocolate fountain.

They were the same colors that we would have seen at my original prom, right down to the theme my class had settled on: A Night in Paris.

"This is amazing," I said.

"I know your friends can't be at this one but I hope this senior prom will make you happy."

My eyes bounced back and forth with his bright emerald glow. My hands cupped the side of his face. I was glad that my heels made my height equal to his as I leaned in and kissed him passionately. I was practically breathless when I pulled back.

"You make me feel like the luckiest girl every day, Liam Alexander."

"It astounds me how much I love you," Liam said.

My forehead leaned in to rest on his, my thumb caressing his cheek.

"That makes two of us," I said.

As if on cue, music began to play from a speaker system I couldn't see.

"Can I have this first dance?" Liam said.

"Always."

As I reached out to take his hand and pull his body close, I could already tell that my face was going to hurt by the end of the night from all the smiling Liam was bringing out in me. At least that was until a deafening crack lifted my chin so that my gaze could investigate the source of the sound.

But my human speed had seconds to process Liam's glazed-over eyes and unnaturally twisted neck. His hand dropped from mine just as his body fell toward the ground.

"Liam!"

I dropped to my knees, desperate to search for any signs of thick veins on his face when, suddenly, the hair on the back of my neck stood up in alert.

"You really don't have very good luck with proms, do you?"

My head lifted to see Thomas standing a foot away from us, holding a beaming Yahtzee smile. I didn't have time to part my lips, let alone scream, before the familiar blackness took over my senses, leaving me vulnerable in every way.

CHAPTER 23

Price of Justice

My eyes blinked open and a small groan escaped my lips as I twisted my stiff neck. Despite my senses becoming aware of the tall, plush chair supporting my body, it took a few seconds for my mind to catch up to my memory.

"Liam?"

"Go fish."

My head turned swiftly toward the sound, meeting the arrogant smirk of Thomas across from me. A sudden chill shot down into my toes. But it was the unexpected accent shift that threw me, which he easily noticed.

"In my last note, did I forget to mention I'm originally from London?" Thomas said with a teasing clench of his teeth.

"Where's Liam?" I asked, ignoring the introduction of his origin.

"Not here," Thomas said.

Where is here? I thought as I began to gaze around the windowless room. It was well lit by dozens of burning candles, which illuminated the square antique table between us. It was as if he were Henry VIII seducing his next wife.

I briefly looked at Thomas's tailored black suit before focusing back on the gaze that was making its way uncomfortably down my body like a serpent.

"I hope you don't mind a few changes I've made. I found them to be more *suitable*."

My body instinctively pulled back into my chair. I gripped the thin arms as I lowered my chin to take in the difference from my former appearance.

My blue prom dress had been swapped for the familiar red one-shoulder dress, while my feet were occupied by black designer heels that had been in the same box Thomas left on my porch. Even my hair was differently styled: down and pushed in front of my shoulders. My stomach twitched and my mouth dried at the thought of Thomas being the one to undress my unconscious body.

"I think it's only fair," Thomas said, rising to his feet. His eyes never left mine as he slowly crept around the table. "Seeing as I *did* go to the trouble of picking each of those items for you."

I didn't dare mention that the black clutch was missing from his sadistic designer collection. Instead, I closed my eyes for a second as he moved to stand behind me. He leaned forward, placing his right hand on my exposed shoulder. His thumb played with my collarbone for a few seconds before his hand begun to trail upward until it was grasping my neck. He held onto my vulnerability as if he possessed it, exhaling with pleasure at my rising heart rate.

"No need to be nervous," Thomas said.

He leaned down, placing his lips close to my neck.

"I mean you no harm."

I knew he was putting on this display not to frighten me but to make a point of his control. He wanted me to know that he didn't need to restrain me. I would have barely risen from my seat before he'd already snapped my neck.

Of course, it wasn't until Thomas had pulled away and come back into view that I released the tension in my shoulders. It was enough to get me to refocus and try studying the room again, desperate for any type of clue that Sean could use. Another chill ran down my spine as the panic of my bouncing gaze was left with nothing but a dead end.

"Give up yet?"

"Where are we?"

"Toronto," Thomas said.

"Really," I asked, confused by his deadpan eyes. Until his facade broke with a tooth-revealing smile.

"No."

Thomas flicked his eyebrows upward in a teasing manner.

"But wouldn't it have been nice if I'd made it that easy?"

I could feel his stare on me as I attempted to relay mental pictures. Regardless of their uselessness, I wanted to convey to Sean that I was trying.

"You know, if that useless Roamer taught me anything with you, it would be knowing how to choose a location. Can't have that brother of yours finding us, right?" He tapped the side of his head with his index finger. "But I must admit, it's cute to see how hard you're trying anyway."

I gulped slightly at the invasive pair of bright grey eyes.

"Despite whatever your plan is with me, Liam won't stop until you're dead," I said.

He narrowed his eyes but his grin remained as he leaned forward with interest—at least for a few seconds, until he suddenly sat back, raising his finger in the air.

"Speaking of," Thomas said with the glee of someone concealing a great surprise, one that was perfectly timed with the ringing of the cellphone sitting near his left hand.

He winked at me while answering the expected caller.

"Hello, Jane."

Not until he held the phone away from his face did I realize that it was a video call. The thought of its purpose caused my anxiety to skyrocket past the already uncomfortable level.

"Thomas," Jane said.

It was odd, almost as if it were a response to her name being called rather than a reciprocated greeting.

"Freshly cracked?"

My brow wrinkled in confusion at Thomas's words, watching as he winked at me once more. The repetitive gesture made me involuntarily grimace.

"Yes," Jane said.

"Excellent. Go ahead and proceed for Emma, then."

Thomas brought the phone back down. It was within full view, but not close enough for me to touch it. I begrudgingly looked down at the phone, immediately understanding their coded meaning. My body stiffened at the sight of Jane hovering over Liam's face with a newly satisfied grin. Liam's neck was broken, leaving him alive but vulnerable. *Freshly cracked.*

"I'm surprised you don't want the honors on this one," Jane said.

"I have what I want."

I could feel Thomas's eyes on me as if what played out didn't matter to him—only my reaction to it. The crack from below caught my full attention. I watched as Liam's head twitched and his neck realigned but only for a moment, until Jane reached down and snapped Liam's neck once again. My stomach clenched at the sight.

"Are you serious?"

She spoke to Thomas but looked back at me with the familiar disgust I remembered from the day I met her. It was the same loathing that came across on Sean's wedding day. I gulped slightly, feeling as if she were playing her part a little *too* well. It was convincing enough to raise my lingering doubt that she had fooled us all.

"You've seen the vulnerable stupidity that this one held from pining after her and you're still willing to play seconds with his toy?"

I lifted my eyes to see Thomas's gaze shifting down toward the phone. All humor had evaporated from his face.

"Don't mistake this convenience of our alliance as an equal partnership, dear Jane. I have no problem terminating it if you question my choices again."

His words were calm but the threat radiated from them.

"Very well," Jane said.

I looked back at the phone. For the first time, I could see the façade drop, her apologetic eyes looking back at me. I knew she was committed to the plan just as much as she had ever been but her empathy brought out a harsh reminder. She was willing to do whatever it took to bring down Thomas. I was starting to get the suspicion that didn't just mean me anymore.

"Wait," I said, shifting upward, trying to get as close to the phone as possible while talking to Thomas. "Please, you can have me but leave him."

Thomas chuckled as my hands lifted to the table. Despite his amusement, my gaze bounced up to him with what I hoped was a plea-filled stare.

"Please," I said in a whispered breath.

"I don't like competition," Thomas said.

"I'll do whatever you ask. I'll stay with you...*willingly*."

"A fair trade." Thomas shifted in his chair as his head tilted back and forth with the temptation. "But what's to stop him from coming for you once he awakens?"

I had no answer to give because even if the words left my lips, there would be no possible way Liam would stop fighting to get to me. Thomas knew that just as much as I did.

"You see, Emma, regardless of your pleas, Liam would never obey any request to leave you with me. It wouldn't benefit me at all to strike this bargain for his life."

"Please," I whispered.

"Jane."

It wasn't a call but a command that Thomas voiced back to the phone. It felt as if I were in a play but hadn't been given the script. All I could think to do was improve the lines and hope that Jane would somehow clue me in to where I was supposed to stand on the stage.

"Jane, I'm sorry about Henry."

As odd as the timing felt, it was still an opportunity to give Jane a sincere apology—one that I'd been looking for a chance to make after Charlie's visit. It couldn't hurt to navigate a truthful topic while I waited on the plan to update.

"You and Charlie should have had the chance to carry out your oath. The Alexanders had no right to intervene."

Finally, Jane looked at the camera, a glistening bright glow of emotion making its way to the surface. She nodded silently with appreciation before mouthing the words, *I'm sorry.*

"Are you done?" Jane said in an irritated tone.

My blood pumped faster as she once again silently mouthed to the camera, *I'm sorry.*

I had wanted an update of the plan but not in that direction. My stomach pulled inward as I realized my instinct had been right about her willing risk. She was loyal to the New Order and determined to bring Thomas to an end. That meant sacrificing Liam in the process.

"Wait...Jane." I wasn't sure if Thomas had noticed but I certainly could hear the difference between any previous acting and my new, anxious tone.

"It's not going to work," I said with a vehement shake of my head. "Jane, it's not worth it. Please, Jane...don't!"

I had never heard such a plea come from my voice but the desperation was raw and determined. She had to know this plan wouldn't work. If she went through with this collateral damage I would never be willing to help her with the next stage of the plan. The deal would be...

"I'm sure you are," Jane said, interrupting my thoughts as she swiftly brought her hand down with a sharp, thick branch and pierced Liam's chest.

"No!"

My lungs felt as if they were inhaling cement. My breaths were labored as I looked away from the phone and down toward the table.

"You got what you wanted, you sick bastard. Now, turn it off!"

Thomas stood, quickly making his way to my side. I flinched at the slow draw of his finger up my arm. I regretted looking away from him as my eyes flickered up to the video in time to see the green flames burning in the background. Thomas lowered his lips just below my jawline, causing me to violently turn my head away.

"I hope you soon burn in hell."

"Thank you," Thomas said to Jane as he picked up the phone from the table.

"My pleasure," Jane replied before ending the call.

"I wonder," Thomas said while coming back into my view. He reached forward with his thumbs to wipe under my eyes. His touch lingered against my skin for seconds, as if he was unable to resist the contact. "Does hell come with an angel like you?"

I felt myself fading into a deep mental abyss. What had I just been a part of? I couldn't even pinpoint the emotion that resonated the most inside of me. It was as if my sadness and anger were spinning on a continuous wheel that refused to stop long enough to pick a winner.

"What do you get out of this anyway?"

He tilted his head, amused by my words.

"You," Thomas said as if it were obvious.

"You have me physically but I'll never be yours willingly."

"And what makes you think I need you willing?" Thomas said.

"Because I'm sure having a pet would be too boring for someone like you. You want someone to cause chaos with. A partner in crime. An obedient slave would never excite you."

The small wink and twitch of his eyebrows told me I had nailed him exactly. He lowered his face, pressing his nose into my hair to inhale my scent. I could feel the lustful smile on his lips as he spoke an inch away from my ear.

"I guess we'll have fun finding out, my pet."

"I have another idea," a familiar voice said.

Thomas and I turned to my left, toward a space that had previously been empty, to find Charlie.

Suddenly, I couldn't remember what they had told me the day we met. I knew Charlie could shift objects but not himself. *Right?* But my confusion was solitary, as the appearance of Charlie didn't faze Thomas at all. In fact, it seemed to amuse him.

"If you're here to carry out your Beta Order on your sister, I'm afraid you've come to the wrong place."

"I'm exactly where I'm supposed to be," Charlie said.

Thomas clapped his palms together as if excited by the idea of playing a game of mental chess with someone else—someone who thought they were good but whom he knew he could easily dominate.

"I see what you've done there. Except for one thing: You aren't in my coven, mate. The only one allowed that right would be my own..." He shrugged as he tilted his head back and forth. "That is, if I hadn't killed them all centuries ago."

"You didn't have a coven. Unless you count your psycho creator and his demented girlfriend."

"Oh man, you caught me." His lips rose to reveal both rows of teeth as he lifted his hands in false surrender. "Well...*did* you catch me, though?"

His eyebrows twitched, as if he were feeding off the stifle of his words. "I mean, just think how pathetic your coven is at this point. You've spent centuries hunting me and I ripped your little family apart with one spear to the heart."

Thomas clapped his hands together in excitement, proud of the death that had started everything. I closed my eyes for a moment, reliving the moment when Katherine's warm blood had splashed onto my face.

When I opened my eyes, I could see Thomas standing tall, walking closer to Charlie, who clenched his fists tightly. I was astounded that he hadn't already charged at the taunt.

"You're a coven of fools," Thomas said as he stood arrogantly close. His next words came out in a terrifyingly low-toned threat. "And I've grown bored of your chases, so I'm going to put a permanent end to your useless Roamer Coven." He paused, tilting his head as if presented with a new idea.

"Consider it my own *Beta Order*."

Despite the new threat to Jane's life too, Charlie grinned while looking over at me as if trying to convey a message. Then he shifted his focus back to Thomas.

"Send my regards to Katherine and Henry."

My throat tightened in helpless fear seconds before Thomas's bare hand punched through Charlie's chest as if it were made of play dough. I knew from what Liam had told me that immortals were similar to the myth of Achilles: invulnerable to any form of fatal attack to their bodies except for the fail-safe skin directly in front of their hearts. Most immortal deaths I had seen were caused by manual weapons but that didn't mean the area was limited to steel and stakes. My guess was that was because those of the New Order had no intention of cruelty or malice. Their only purpose was duty and, therefore, they preferred quickly-made weapons that assisted with swift and considerately clean deaths.

But then there were those immortals who chose to indulge in their sadistic pleasures, extinguishing any remaining light of morality that might linger. Fiona had done so on the boat when she sank her teeth into Erika's neck without remorse—a sadistic act that I suspected she learned directly from the immortal who was looking down at his bloody hand with a satisfied grin. It was as if Thomas were gazing at a perfectly picked apple from a tree instead of the dripping red mass that had been Charlie's heart.

My arms moved to protectively grip my stomach as Thomas turned back to me. He lifted the bloody heart victoriously before carelessly letting it roll from his fingers. It landed near Charlie's head, which was turned in my direction, allowing me to easily see the signs of immediate decay that formed with his large, exposed veins.

Thomas's chuckle of amusement at my shock was irritatingly painful. His stare remained on me as his clean hand reached for the white handkerchief tucked into his suit jacket pocket. He began to wipe the blood from his hand purposely slow, relishing my discomfort.

My shoulders pulled back in stiffened defense when he uncharacteristically dropped the linen cloth prematurely to the ground. I watched him drop to his knees. For the first time since I had known him, the shift of his stoic bright eyes conveyed a new, confused fear.

My gaze remained frozen as Lillian suddenly appeared in front of Thomas, her arm extended into his chest with a piece of sharp metal.

"How's that for a coven of fools?" Lillian said in a venomous tone.

Thomas fell backward in unexpected defeat, his feet touching the last victim he would ever claim. I looked up to see Lillian's stare, both of us remaining silent. Once again, the wheel of emotions was spinning. Instead of stopping, it merely added another category of shock.

I tried to remind myself that Thomas's reign of terror was over. I tried to celebrate that the plan I had agreed to had worked. I tried to keep repeating that the victory of his death meant a safer world for my kind. The only problem was that another repetitive thought kept overshadowing the others.

Yes, but at what cost?

CHAPTER 24

Aftershock

The moment the immortal skin of their bodies hit the flame, the fire burned with a green glow. I looked up toward Lillian as she cautiously approached.

"Why are you always the one saving me?" I joked in a sardonic tone.

"What else are friends for?"

The venom was gone from her voice, once again replaced by her usual casual teasing as she lifted a finger in the air.

"Sit tight for a moment. I need to make contact with Jane."

My head snapped over as she spoke Jane's name. It was as if the word triggered a spell, compromising my memories. I tried to close my eyes as the adrenaline rushed through me but the image of Liam dying by Jane's hands made my own hands shake.

It was as if an implant had been inserted into my brain, signaling a mute button for the environment around me, though not because something was physically wrong. No bomb had gone off, affecting my senses. My mind had merely gone into a state of shock.

My breaths were becoming uneven. Before I realized what I was doing I felt my legs moving. My body was like that of a sluggish zombie, making its way to the opposite corner of the room. I sat on the ground, throwing my gifted heels in an unknown direction before bringing my knees into my chest. I wrapped my arms around my legs, focusing on the floor as I rocked back and forth.

"She killed him," I breathed out in a barely audible whisper.

I could hear myself repeating the words but was unable to force myself to stop. Lillian's voice was a mere echo underwater.

Just when I thought my mind would give in to the darkness, a sound broke through with perfect clarity. It was like breaking the surface of a thick, endless fog. The spell of my trapped mind was broken at the sound of one voice.

"Emma."

The sounds around me rose in volume as I looked up to see Liam from across the room. I stood without hesitation, allowing my feet to lead me forward in quick steps until my legs urged them to produce faster results.

I launched into Liam's body and his arms instinctively held me with a protective strength. I pushed my body closer to his own, if that were possible. My face pressed into the safe crook of his neck. My throat burned but I was unable to hold back the new release of tears. It was hard to determine whether their agenda was led by fear or relief.

His right arm held my body against his while the left gently ran along the back of my head.

"I'm here, love. I'm here."

I pulled back, gently tracing the outline of his face, imprinting it to memory as if readying myself for it to disappear. He used his thumbs to gently wipe away the escaped tears that continued to run down my face.

"How many times must I be forced to think you're dead?"

"I hope never again."

Liam's voice was a whisper, releasing his own vulnerable relief. It was hard to tell whether he was speaking to me or releasing a small hopeful plea to the higher beings responsible for creating immortals. It inspired me enough to speak my own truth.

"I think if my heart goes through the pain of losing you again, it might rupture and kill me."

"And that very sight would cause my own to rupture."

I leaned in to his forehead, letting the warmth of his skin comfort me back to a calm reality.

"Let's get out of here," Lillian said.

"Yes," Liam agreed, taking my hand and entwining it with his own.

We followed slightly behind Lillian, who stopped in front of what I had assumed was a dead-end wall. She lifted her hand to a small beige panel and flipped it open to reveal a small black button. Once she pressed it, the wall opened by way of a carved-out, framed sliding door, revealing a stone staircase behind it.

"Come on," Lillian said as she headed up the staircase.

Without hesitation, Liam swooped down to lift me off my feet and into his arms. He took off up the stairs. Within a few seconds, he was placing me next to Lillian.

"Thanks," I said.

I reached out for his hand again just as Lillian was palming a black box to her right. At the sound of the click, the door in front of us unlocked, which allowed her to easily push it open using the exposed silver bar.

From the moment the door left the frame, I was hit by the sound of honking horns, ambulance sirens, and the hustle of bustling city life. It was a series of sounds carefully shielded from the interior of the building we had just exited.

There was a slight breeze but the temperature was comfortable as my eyes looked up at the cityscape, quite aware of Thomas's location once I saw the famous tourist landscape.

"It's a shame we don't have more time," Lillian joked in the distance. "I love New York."

I smirked, already feeling the adrenaline wearing off and the exhaustion catching up with me. I squeezed Liam's hand while looking up to meet his gaze.

"Let's go home."

CHAPTER 25

Baited

My mind began to wake, pulling me from my slumber by the touch of Liam's tender kiss against my forehead.

"Emma."

I felt the tickle of his lips move near my ear as he beckoned me with a whispered call of my name. His hand soothed the side of my head, gently rubbing his thumb around my temple.

"We're about to land, love."

With his warning, my eyes blinked open obediently. I stretched my arms and took in the environment of the private cabin. I sat in a readied position as I looked out the window, noticing our slow descent into a small airport.

The last thing I had remembered was following Lillian up another staircase that was attached to a chartered jet. I climbed the six steps without asking questions, making my way to one of the beige leather seats. Within seconds of reclining and shutting my eyes, a blanket was being placed on my body. Not long after, I drifted off into a welcome sleep.

"Welcome back," Lillian joked.

I had just enough time to sleepily smirk at her before I had to sit back in my seat and brace myself for the landing. My body jerked slightly as the wheels touched down but Liam instinctively held out his arm to prevent my body from lurching forward. Once we began to taxi, I turned to Liam with the resurfaced curiosity I had left back in New York.

"What airport are we at?"

"New Bern," Liam said. "My car is already parked here from when I flew out."

Though the plane was still taxiing, Lillian stood and walked down the aisle toward the cabin door.

"I'll bring the car," she said.

Liam reached into his pocket and threw his keys across the plane into Lillian's waiting hand. As the wheels came to a halt, she swiftly reached up to pull down the red release lever. I was certain the stairs had barely unfolded to the ground before she jumped out of the opening and disappeared.

My gaze was soon distracted by Liam's extended hand. I looked up at his waiting bright emerald gaze and patient grin. I reached up to meet his grasp, letting him pull me to my feet. Instinctively, I smoothed out my red dress as Liam stepped back and turned his body to give me enough room to walk ahead of him. I looked down for a few seconds, unable to resist the sardonic humor of my wardrobe.

"I imagine if Lillian knew that the prom dress she chose would have such back luck attached to it, she would have gone in another direction."

Liam chuckled loudly as we made our way down the aisle toward the opening.

"Don't think that thought didn't cross her mind as she followed you to New York."

Despite the humorous tone his words held, I turned back to see the serious undertone within his tense jaw. I opened my mouth but immediately paused as I watched his body language convey the same message of his stare. His hands shifted out, as if preparing to be used as buffers when he studied the stairs ahead of me. I knew he was trying to silence my curiosity for a moment, at least until I made it down the steps in my heels.

I turned to reach out for the small handrail before cautiously making my way down the few steps of the plane. Lillian was already waiting for us, leaning against Liam's maroon BMW, which she had pulled a few feet from the jet.

She smiled at the sight of me, as if she hadn't already seen me minutes before. I had to admit, it was contagious as I walked toward her with similarly risen cheeks.

"I'm glad to see you looking better," Lillian said.

As with Liam, her tone was full of humor but her eyes studied me with genuine concern. My mind flashed back to the odd behavior she must have witnessed in New York.

"I'm sorry for—"

"No, Emma," she said, interrupting me as she opened the passenger door. Once I was inside the car, she swiftly moved back to the driver's seat just as Liam found the seat next to me in the back. "With all that you had been through, it was perfectly understandable to go into that state of shock. It was inevitable."

My arm slid over to clasp Liam's hand with a tight squeeze.

"Thinking Liam is dead seems to have that effect on me," I said while bouncing my eyes to my lap, instantly feeling Liam's reciprocated squeeze. "I'm just glad it wasn't more than a few minutes or it might have looked worse than..."

My voice trailed off as I looked up at the review mirror to meet Lillian's gaze, which had quickly shifted over to Liam with a furrowed brow of hesitancy.

"What?" I said, turning my head to look between the two siblings.

"Emma," Lillian said, calling back my attention to the mirror. "I tried getting through to you for three hours. Nothing I said or did could pull you back to reality. In fact, you were so far deep in that state that I began to worry even Liam's presence wouldn't be enough."

"Oh." My head pulled back, my eyes bouncing around the car to avoid her waiting stare. "That's..." I shook my head, not sure how to process the oddity of my behavior.

"She called me to advise Jane to stay back and not join me on the flight," Liam said.

I lifted my head to look over at Liam, pulling my lips inward with an embarrassed shrug.

"I guess I finally cracked."

My eyebrows twitched as if trying to make fun of myself in the hopes of taking off some of the underlining concern. But the best way to do that was to simply change the subject.

"Alright, so now that I'm of *sane* mind, can either of you explain what part of the plan I was obviously not a part of?"

"Emma." Lillian paused a few seconds, chewing on her bottom lip as if that helped her process her own emotions of the last 24 hours. "Listen, I know being a human in our world has never been an easy road for you. And while it might show cause to prevent relationships like Liam's and yours, I want you to know that I'm sorry for what we've put you through, especially these past five months."

I sighed while holding a small grin as I easily read between her words. *I love you too, Lil.*

"I know," I said.

Liam remained silent but I noticed how he kept a firm grip on my hand, as if unwilling to break our link. Lillian's lips twitched slightly, her eyes meeting mine as she spoke.

"We should start from the moment she put her plan in motion," Lillian said.

"You mean when she showed up at the house?"

"No," Lillian said while shaking her head. "*Before* she met with any of us."

"Wait, so you mean..." My eyes narrowed as I tilted my head in contemplation. "Her plan was already in the works *with our without* my agreement?"

"She had already sent Charlie to Marius to alert him of her proposal. By the time she showed up at the house, her proposal had been accepted."

"Meaning her plan involved baiting two people," I said with a higher-pitched irritation.

Both immortals in the car were silent as if the question were rhetorical. My eyes closed briefly and I released a small chuckle of disbelief at Jane's manipulation.

"Did you know?"

My chest felt tight as I waited for Liam and his sister to admit if the Alexanders were involved in putting my life on the line before I had even agreed to it.

"No," Liam said.

I looked over to see the vehement shake of his head as his free hand took mine with a needful grasp.

"Jane kept her full plan carefully hidden because most of it counted on *our* authentic reactions to events surrounding you. Meaning, if you'd said no that day when she asked you to risk it all, we'd have stood behind you."

It hit me that Jane must have been using her power in the house to shield Sean from her *full* plan. My brother's reaction was bad enough to what he *did* know. I couldn't imagine his fury if he had known the truth.

I pulled my hands out of Liam's only so that I could carry out my agenda to take away the distress radiating off him. I ran my fingers through his blond hair before slipping them down to hold the sides of his face.

"But she knew I wouldn't say no," I said. It was a declaration to myself rather than to Liam.

I turned my head to Lillian, willing her to continue while my body remained close to Liam's with a deep need for his contact.

"Jane had ordered Charlie to follow a newly created pair that Thomas sent to you and your friends."

"Fiona and Ben," I said, shaking my head at another fond memory I would be lucky to keep.

"Jane knew they believed they were invulnerable under Thomas's rule and therefore wouldn't suspect eyes on them."

"Not surprising," I said. "They did come across as believing that they were easily untouchable."

Liam's thumb soothed the back of my hand as Lillian spoke.

"Inevitably, he watched them arguing over the new order given by Thomas to carry out a kill on their friend, Fredrick."

My back stiffened.

"The same Fredrick who tried to kill me?"

"Yes," Lillian confirmed.

"Well, it seems someone lost that argument because he came flying through the window. Did Thomas trust them to leave the note too?"

Trusting someone with such an intimate task didn't seem to be in Thomas's nature. Lillian's head shake confirmed that.

"Charlie said they dropped his dead body at Thomas's feet and waited for their next order but…"

"What?"

"Thomas thanked them for the task and then killed them."

"Why?" I asked with a furrowed brow.

"Because of the night on the boat. They were meant to scare you, not leave you for dead."

There was still an underlining bitterness toward Jane but I couldn't ignore the fact that she was right about the escalation of Thomas's obsession with me. It was terrifying to know that he probably would have snapped the neck of his best friend if they had attempted to inflict any harm on me.

"Does that mean Thomas was watching us after he threw Fredrick through the window?"

Lillian nodded.

"It was that need to watch his own chaos that gave Jane the distracted moment she required to leave Charlie with his next order."

"I assume that was the reason for his drop-in visit," I said

"Yes, to give us as much as possible."

If getting one line of the whole play is as much as possible, then sure.

"Do you realize that most of this plan relied on both my fear and yours?" I said, looking between Lillian and Liam. "Because knowing I was going to be kidnapped doesn't seem to be something that even immortals like you could easily digest. Certainly not Sean. But I'm sure Jane loved having his heightened emotion for upselling the bait, right?"

I looked out the window, observing the green leaves occupying the trees along the highway. I chewed on my lip for a few seconds of silence before turning my focus back to the patient immortals sharing the drive with me.

"Sorry," I said.

"You don't have to apologize for processing all of this," Liam said.

"So, what was Charlie's next order?"

"From that point on, he was ordered to watch you and wait until Thomas made his move. Once you were taken, he was to reach out to the one Alexander with the asset of invisibility."

"You," I said.

"Yes. While in pursuit, he called me. I caught up with him mid-route. Once we approached the airport, I cloaked him and myself, which allowed us to slip onto his plane. The hardest part was…"

Lillian paused, her hands gripping the steering wheel with a curved tension.

"The hardest part was standing there helplessly with you lying unconscious a few feet away from me."

"That couldn't have been easy," I said, trying not to think about the way he had managed to keep me unconscious during the flight. "But at least you made up for it in the end, right?"

I'm glad she caught on to my slight tease, which caused her to shake her head and playfully wipe the back of her hand across her forehead. All the pieces connected except for one, which still pulled at my stomach. It was the very reason that had caused me to go into a catatonic state.

My eyes shifted to my hands, which had made their way back into my lap. Slowly, I found the courage to lift my head to meet my boyfriend's eyes with a questioning gaze.

"Why did the plan have to involve me believing she had to *actually* kill you…" My voice faded as I attempted to hide the thickness of my throat. I shook my head as if that would keep any tears from falling.

"Like you were just some collateral damage that was necessary to the plan?"

"She wanted that reassurance for Charlie and Lillian that his further distraction would come from the purity of your devastation at my death. I didn't even know what was happening because she kept snapping my neck to keep me from regaining consciousness."

Shit. My mind thought back to the moment when I had been watching the video. Her acting and careful video framework had fooled me enough that I didn't notice the fatal stab had been slightly off-camera. *Clever bitch.*

"It wasn't until I woke up to the flames burning a body— one belonging to another lackey of Thomas's—that she explained what she had done."

The longer he spoke on the memory, the more I heard the pent-up anger in Liam's voice.

"Why wouldn't she have looped you in from the moment she found you?"

"Because she didn't want to risk the plan's failure due to false mistrust."

I knew that meant Jane didn't want to risk wasting time by having to explain her scheme to my brother. So, instead, she took Liam from the dance floor and hid him from the others until the plan had been fully carried out and completed.

"I think a large part of her knew that if I woke up and she told me she needed me to *die* in front of you on camera, I'd resist and probably snap her neck in the process."

"Really?"

"I wouldn't put you through that again, no matter what was at stake," Liam said.

My head leaned in, meeting his and letting us both reset from the anger Jane had caused for a mere assurance. I lingered in silence with Liam, trying to dissect my thoughts. Yes, I understood Jane's agenda to a point, and yet it still made me uneasy to know that she had baited me not just physically but emotionally as well.

"I'm sorry, Emma," Lillian said.

I sighed to the break of silence, pulling back to merely nod.

"Do you think Charlie knew he was going to die?"

Unlike dealing with the anger of being manipulated over Liam, Charlie's death was painfully real. The image of seeing his heart lying next to his body played like a loop in my brain. Liam reached up to run his hands through my hair, the sorrow lingering in his touch.

"We knew we'd have only one shot," Lillian said sadly. "Because the only thing that would bring about Thomas's downfall was the element of surprise. We both knew that was going to come only from one of us being a sacrifice. But I think…" Lillian's fingers tapped against the steering wheel. "I think Charlie made that choice when he was sent to meet with Marius. I could sense it from the moment he stepped out of my touch."

"Yeah," I said, nodding in agreement. "Something about the way he looked at me too before he died told me he knew there was no other way." I spoke as if I was coming to a realization while remembering the brief moment. "It was like he knew it had to be him."

"I think in the end, despite Thomas's cruel intention behind the words, Charlie was elated at the thought of seeing Katherine and Henry again," Lillian said.

My head titled in thought at Charlie's willing sacrifice.

"Do you think he was so willing because he knew that taking out Thomas would fulfill the purpose that their coven has been pursuing for so many centuries?"

"Maybe," Lillian said "But regardless, it was an honor to know him. A true honor."

I leaned my head back against the seat and let out a heavy sigh that I had been holding deep within for five months, if not longer.

"It's over."

My words came out in a whisper before I exhaled with a small laugh. I lifted my head to look at Liam apologetically.

"Sorry. It's just hitting me, you know? I've been terrified for five *long* months. And even though I don't think I'll be able to look Jane in the face for a while without wanting to slap her…" I paused, shaking my head. "It doesn't take away the fact that we won. We actually pulled this off."

"We did," Liam said.

"I feel like I can finally come up for air," I said.

"You were a great sport," Lillian said.

"What do I get for that?" I teased.

"To graduate high school," Lillian bantered back.

As odd as that may have sounded, it was a major prize after truly believing I wouldn't live to see it. I smiled up at her with a slight nod of approval.

"Fair enough. But I have one last question."

Lillian's brow rose with expectation, her eyes meeting mine in the mirror.

"Am I the only one who didn't know Thomas was British?"

The car filled with laughter. For the first time in months, I felt as if the anchor tied around my leg had suddenly come loose, letting me rise to the surface. The thought allowed the left side of my mouth to curl triumphantly with the light-hearted moment.

I laid my head against Liam's shoulder and looked out the window with the grateful hope that came from the sun rising on a new day.

CHAPTER 26

Messenger

"Morning."

My lips curved at the sound of Liam's voice welcoming me into consciousness. I loved the way he could always sense that my body was awake before I did.

"Morning," I said.

"How did you sleep?"

Liam leaned down to tenderly kiss my shoulder, causing my eyes to close as I absorbed the peaceful bliss. Once I began to turn over, I felt his arm adjust upward in perfect sync with my body until I was comfortable. My hand instinctively lifted to meet his face, my thumb outlining his cheekbone as my eyes took in the beauty of the immortal who stared back adoringly at me.

"Honestly, this is the best night's sleep I've had since…" My eyes shifted to my hand. Suddenly, I was aware of how difficult it still was to voice my pain aloud.

"Since I disappeared," Liam said. His concerned voice was low but there wasn't an inflection that addressed it as a question. It was as if he was attempting to fight off his guilt. He placed a piece of hair behind my ear, slowly letting his knuckles drag along my jawline.

I nodded in silent agreement but was eager to escape the sorrow that the moment had caused. It would be easy to drown in the nightmare of events that had occurred since I met Liam. But if I had learned anything, it was to enjoy the victory of the good parts more.

"What time is your Watch?"

"In an hour," Liam said.

"Plenty of time to celebrate," I said with a mischievous grin.

The sound of his chuckle gave way to his amusement before he moved in to lay his lips on my left cheek.

"What are we celebrating exactly?"

I giggled at the feel of his playful kisses making their way down my neck. "Well, if we start from when shit turned bad, we could say that getting you back alive is one."

"Good reason," Liam said as his lips traveled along my jawline.

"Or how about ending Thomas's reign of terror and still making it to graduation?"

Liam lifted his head, carrying the crooked smirk I knew all too well.

"Technically, graduation is in two days, so—"

I cut him off with a long, passionate kiss. He pulled back, taking in the sight of my face. I loved the way he looked at me and I always would. Though I didn't say it aloud, Liam's love was definitely another reason to feel grateful.

"You're right, still plenty to celebrate," Liam said as his lips pressed into mine.

Hours later, I still held my satisfied grin while I cruised down the backroad highway.

"Why are you smiling like the Cheshire cat?"

Instantly, I brought my lips together, forgetting about my friend. After Liam left my room, I had sent Michael a text to see if he wanted to join me on a spontaneous drive.

"Maybe I'm just happy we're about to graduate."

I shrugged, turning my smile on Michael, who rolled his eyes.

"I'll pretend that was the reason but..." He paused, his lips turning inward, and nodded as if in agreement with himself. "I must admit, it's pretty nuts that high school is over."

I reached over to turn up the volume of the speakers.

"It is nuts to think it's finally over," I said as I joined Michael in a karaoke car ride, getting lost in teenage bliss as we belted out along with the radio. It was a feeling that had been foreign the past couple of months—a rare moment of normalcy I hoped to catch up on over the summer before he headed off to Georgia in the fall.

I was still smiling with a childlike grin as I turned down the radio. "Can you reach my purse from the back?"

"Yeah, hold on," Michael said while taking off his seatbelt, instantly causing my eyes to roll.

"I just wanted some gum. It's not important enough to endanger your life, idiot."

"Relax, it's no big deal." He smiled innocently before bouncing back into his seat and dramatically pulling his seatbelt across his body until it clicked. "See?"

"Don't judge me for being concerned about your safety."

If he knew the truth about my life, he wouldn't be so careless either.

"I'm fine, *Mom*."

"Jerk," I said, unable to resist an amused smirk.

"A jerk who risked his life for this prize," Michael said while teasingly dangling the flat strip surrounded by foil.

"Alright, thanks for being so *noble*. May I have my gum now, good honorable sir?"

"I'll think about it," Michael said before bending forward to turn the radio back up.

"Jerk," I said again but out of the corner of my eye, I could already see him holding the piece of gum near my face.

Without looking away from the road, I lifted my right palm to him. At least that was until within, a blink's time, I retracted my hand to the steering wheel to assist the other. The gum was forgotten as I took in the red-haired female suddenly standing in the middle of the road.

She stood indifferent to the obstacle in her path before she disappeared altogether. Instinct caused my foot to shift over to my brake pedal, as I was desperate to pull over and regain my composure. I wasn't sure if it was a long-overdue PTSD moment but I needed some air regardless.

My foot had barely begun to linger on the pedal when the woman I had imagined in my head reappeared within a foot of my car.

"Oh shi—"

The redhead threw down her hand with purpose, colliding with the hood of my Jetta. The unexpected force threw the car into a vertical rise forward before it flipped into an air roll, then landed brutally on the pavement with two rolls until it came to a stop upside down and perpendicular to the road.

I gasped with a harsh breath, pain beginning to flood in slowly and then all at once. Unlike with prom, this type of pain was nearly impossible to pinpoint in any one direction. I could feel a warmth, both on my face and in my scalp. I had to keep blinking, as my vision could pick up only a blur of my surroundings.

It was hard to tell how much time was passing but finally my eyes were able to focus so that I could look for something. *Michael,* I thought as my mind caught up with my vision. Slowly, I turned my head to check on Michael in the passenger seat only to be left in a panic at his absence.

"Michael?"

My voice was weak. It was hard to tell if the call was audible.

"I wouldn't worry about your friend."

I could hear the crunch of broken glass as steps neared the passenger door. The vibration of the car caused my head to turn the other way, listening as my car was ripped apart by a bulldozer's force.

I felt the exposed breeze before I turned my head to take in what had once been the right side of my Jetta. A pair of legs occupying black jeans appeared and squatted until they revealed a thin, short woman with long, dark hair. I could have sworn the woman on the road had red hair. *Didn't she?* Regardless, the bright glow of this woman's immortal blue eyes told me this wouldn't end well.

"I'm sure your human body is in a lot of pain. And as much fun as it would be to see you die, it won't be half as fun as getting to see what happens next."

Her words were confusing but that didn't stop me from taking the opportunity to satisfy my curiosity.

"Are you getting revenge for Thomas?"

I should have known it wouldn't have been that easy to slay Thomas. Surely, he would have had his own contingency plans, even in death. How foolish we were to not see that. The woman merely laughed as if she were watching a small toddler attempting to walk for the first time. Maybe I was missing something. Or maybe my curiosity in the midst of my weakness simply amused her.

"What should we do with the spare?"

My focus slipped to the second voice as my head turned enough to see a sight that sent a bucket of ice into my veins. There was the redhead I had seen before. She was standing over Michael's unconscious body, which must have flown out of the car during the crash. Even with the distance, the girl held a familiar face but I couldn't quite understand why.

"What spare?"

The brunette didn't speak, as if confused, but was giving a hidden command to the redhead looming over Michael. The curled lips and gleeful satisfaction radiating off the redhead forced me to turn my head back to the brunette with determination.

"Wait," I said while groaning out with pain. "He's not a part of this…" I paused briefly as if struggling to the surface for a quick breath. "He doesn't know about any of you."

"Shh."

She tapped her polished finger gently against my lips.

"Please don't," I pleaded with a small shake of my head. "Just let him—"

"Go?"

"Please."

"Okay," the brunette said with a nod.

She reached down to maternally smooth my cheek before turning her focus back to her companion. I followed her gaze to see the redhead squatting on Michael's right side, cradling his head just as he began to stir.

"Em…Emma?"

Michael attempted to speak between ragged breaths but my name was all that surfaced. Though he had yet to see me, I attempted a weak smile anyway.

"No feeding."

I squinted with confusion at the out-of-place words but my attention remained on Michael and the redhead who held his head between her palms.

Within one short breath, the redhead's next action left me frozen in disbelief. Despite the immortal speed of the act, I knew the sound all too well. It was the sound of a human neck breaking.

"No…no…" Finally, my mind came back to reality as I turned to look at the dark-haired woman hovering over me. "You said you'd let him go."

"And I did," the brunette said with a smile.

I could feel my hands shaking, but whether out of fear or anger, I wasn't sure. My breaths were becoming heavy as my mind ventured into shock.

"You're welcome."

My eyes closed involuntarily for a few seconds before opening to see the lingering smirk she had yet to drop.

"Who…are you?" I asked through labored breaths.

"I've gone by many names."

She spoke in a fond tone that seemed to be swimming in the blissful times of her past. She traced the outlines of my face with the back of her index finger as she continued. "I was particularly fond of the century I spent as Tatiana. Nothing like hearing humans use it to beg for their meaningless lives once I grew bored of them. *Tatiana, please. Tatiana why? But Tatiana, I love you.*"

The immortal woman laughed cruelly, clearly amused by the fear and infatuation she had elicited from her former victims.

"You're a psychopath."

Her bright blue eyes danced around with a focus on mine as she lowered her face close. Her hand inched around the front of my neck, threatening to squeeze like a serpent at her will. Her smile made it obvious that the gesture wasn't out of anger but enjoyment of my previous words. Thomas wasn't the only one who loved to play games, it seemed.

"Without a doubt," the dark-haired immortal confirmed.

"Just kill me already," I said.

"Why do you assume that's what I want?"

Her head tilted and her eyebrows raised in challenge.

"Isn't it?"

"You, dear one," she said, brushing away the few strands of hair that were not dampened by my blood. "Will be my messenger."

"For what?"

She moved to place her lips close to my ear.

"All in good time."

Before I could even think to ask the meaning, I watched as she readily tore her blouse, as if careless of any modesty. Her hand moved swiftly, using a small piece of glass from the ground to slice across the left side of her chest. She moved her body above my openly wounded right hand, allowing gravity to do her bidding.

I commanded my body to fight but it was a useless struggle. Even if I had the strength to fight, it was too late. Her blood had made contact with mine and I had a few seconds head start before my mouth opened involuntarily and my throat released a scream.

I could see the woman grinning in pleasure as the acid of pain spread in every direction that my bloodstream would allow. Nowhere was safe and there was no place to escape.

"See you on the other side, Emma."

She winked before disappearing, leaving me with the open road that was bouncing with the nightmare of my screams. The nightmare of what I knew was happening.

The very risk I had taken with Liam had caught up to me. Mary had always predicted it and fate was finally here to collect payment.

I couldn't bear to imagine Sean helplessly discovering that there was no fix this time. My life was ending whether we accepted it or not. So, before I gave in completely, I pushed one last coherent thought to my brother.

See you on the other side.

About the Author

Jennifer has studied Creative Writing and Literature, and lives in Nashville, Tennessee. To find out more about Jennifer or to learn about updates of her novels you can visit, www.jenniferdean.net.

*Here's a sneak peek at another title by
Jennifer Dean,
I've Been Looking for You*

1

Portland was the latest victim caught within my father's nomadic web. A place I already pitied. Why? Because just like the others, no amount of lure would ever be enough. The coastal town of Maine was set up for failure from the moment we crossed the town line.

The only difference this time was when the clock ran out, and it was time to move on to the next unlucky place, I would no longer be forced to begrudgingly follow. My cheeks rose triumphantly at the reminder as I made my way down the hall. I slung my jacket onto my arms, grateful that my ten years of patience had finally reached it's reward. Yes, in six months, I would graduate and then finally be free.

"Should I make myself scarce by the time you come home with your latest conquest," my father teased as he appeared from around the corner of the kitchen, curiously following my movement toward the front door.

"What makes you think I'm bringing someone home, tonight," I said while reaching behind my neck to flip my long, brown locks out from my jacket's trap.

I held a squinted gaze toward the man, who it felt had become more of a traveling roommate than a father, over the years. He lifted his left hand to scratch the unshaven whiskers that had lazily grown out the past couple of days before his lips rose upward into a crooked know-it-all smirk.

"Well, don't worry, I'm sure by the time I'm back you'll be passed out on the couch," I said looking down toward the beer he held protectively in his right hand before back up to meet his exhausted, hazel eyes with a teasing flick of my eyebrows. The smugness lingered in my risen cheeks as I stepped out of the apartment, pulling the door closed behind me before he could voice any brewing comeback.

I walked across the parking lot, grateful for the windless night as my mind began to drift into the eagerness of my future. I chewed my bottom lip absentmindedly as I danced the line between excitement and fear of the new control I would soon be given. I had pushed down the hope for so long that I wasn't sure I knew how to welcome it back into my life.

It wasn't until I heard the small splash of choppy water that I realized how far my feet had been blindly exploring the streets of Portland. I looked up with intrigue to see the part of town I had ventured into, nodding as if giving approval while continuing toward one of the empty wooden benches. Each one was held within a spotlight glow, thanks to the bulbous lampposts that were evenly spaced down the boardwalk.

I sighed, taking a seat, as I reached into my jacket pocket, pulling out my cheap green, plastic lighter and a newly bought pack of cigarettes. It wasn't a habit I particularly felt addicted to but an activity that I always welcomingly embraced. A treat that offered occasional release.

I squinted, taking in the barely visible glow of the water in front of me as I swiftly placed a cigarette loosely between my lips, tilting my head habitually before igniting the end. I closed my eyes with my inhale, feeling the tension temporarily slide off my shoulders as the nicotine rushed its way into my blood vessels. At least, that was until the sudden sound of footsteps caused me to snap my eyelids back open and reluctantly abandon my new calm. My lips blew out an exhale of smoke, letting my gaze watch it slowly drift up into the air as if being beckoned by the night sky.

I sighed heavily in hopes the person deciding to disturb my serenity would rethink their approach once they heard the sound that displayed their unwanted presence. Unfortunately, I knew I got the opposite effect when the bench creaked in protest of another body's weight.

I brought the cigarette back to my lips as I turned my neck to take in the unwanted guest with an impatient glare. It was a cute blonde dressed in brown designer boots, a charcoaled pea coat, and a white, knitted beanie that matched a pair of gloves. Despite my annoyance, it would've been a lie to say her long flowing locks, flawless ivory skin, and shapely pink lips weren't worth the glance. My mouth opened slightly to release another puff of smoke as my lips twisted with amusement at the way the blonde held her nervous gaze toward the ground.

"You know there are about twenty other empty benches to choose from, right?"

My words caused her to lift her chin, along with her gaze to reveal a pair of piercing, ocean blue eyes that involuntarily caused my chest to tighten.

"Can I have one of those?" The blonde asked softly.

I felt a chill run down my spine that wasn't caused by the cold air as I subtly shook my head to escape the shocked state she had unexpectedly created within me. I held my cigarette loosely between my fingers as my left eyebrow rose once my mind registered her request.

"You sure?"

"Yeah," the blonde politely confirmed.

I tilted my head, watching as she fidgeted uncomfortably with my few seconds of silence.

"You don't seem like the smoking type."

"How would you know?" The girl asked with narrowed eyes.

"Just a hunch," I said with a crooked smirk.

"I could smoke all the time, for all you know."

"Oh yeah," I said unable to resist a chuckle from my challenging tone as I watched the blonde delicately remove the glove from her right hand.

"Can I have one or not?"

I pinched my lips together to hold back my amusement of her growing temper before pulling another cigarette out from my pack and placing into her waiting hand. Now that she had succeeded, her confidence began to waver, causing her to shift her gaze from her palm over to my lite cigarette with uncertainty.

"Something wrong?"

"I don't have—"

"You mean an experienced smoker like yourself doesn't have her own lighter?"

I shook my head mockingly before reaching back into my pocket and pulling out my own once again. I flicked my thumb effortlessly, noticing the curiosity of the blonde as I ignited the flame. My attention was drawn into her beautifully tense jaw before up to watch her blue eyes newly focus on the end of the cigarette she had placed cautiously between her lips.

My resistance to hold off a chuckle failed as her attempt to inhale lasted but two seconds before her truth was revealed. Immediately, she began to cough and flail her hands in the air—as if it would help her control her breathing back to normal.

"You alright?"

She nodded between coughs until she caught her breath.

"Smoke all the time, huh?" I said smiling with a raised eyebrow.

"Okay, so you were right. I've never smoked a day in my life."

"Shocker," I said.

"What does that mean?"

"To be honest, you weren't too hard to peg, Princess," I said turning my head to avoid blowing my exhale of smoke into her face.

"Don't call me that," she said defensively.

"Uh-oh," I said with a fake pout. "Did I strike a nerve, princess?"

"You don't know me," the blonde said with a glare that was accompanied by a soft, insecure voice.

I looked up to the sky with a resisted eye roll as I took one last inhale before tossing my cigarette to the ground. My foot moved to stomp over it with a quick routine twist of my shoe before turning my body around to face the blonde squarely.

"Let me guess, you live in a nice big house with Mommy and Daddy who buy you anything you want. Including a closet full of designer clothes," I paused, slowing eyeing the blonde's outfit, twitching my eyebrows up in challenge as I met her uneasy stare. "And a nice, shiny new car—you probably got the second you turned sixteen, right?" I winked arrogantly, unable to stop the rise of my unprovoked venom. "You date the most popular boy in school." I shrugged my shoulders. "But you still find the need to rebel because life just isn't fair when Daddy makes you have a curfew."

"You're an asshole," the blonde said.

"Tell me it isn't true," I challenged, leaning my temple against my left fist.

The blonde rose to her feet, throwing the cigarette angrily to the ground before stomping off into the direction of the distant parking lot.

"Say hi to Daddy for me," I said before leaning over to pick up her lit leftover and place it between my lips.

Once the silence settled into the air I felt a sting of regret surface from my harsh words. What had the blonde done to get such judgement besides invade my privacy at the wrong time? Perhaps if she would have found me a few hours from now I would have been more inclined to show her my seductive flirty side instead of the asshole version she had encountered.

I shrugged my shoulders with an inhale as I moved to stretch out against the bench, resting my head where the blonde had previously sat. I closed my eyes, ready to take advantage of my solitude only to be met with a familiar pair of ocean blue eyes. I could feel a playful grin rise beyond my lips at the hope of getting to see them again.

MAY 18, 2015

3:40 p.m.

Most people were grateful to wake up from their nightmares but I preferred them. Maybe that was because my real life was far worse than any hell my mind could imagine.

"Damn, they keep sending em' younger and younger."

My hands dropped to my lap as my gaze lifted up from my navy blue, slip-on shoes to see a woman with long, curly brown hair making her way into the small, square cell with a familiarity I envied. I subtly bounced my eyes around her wrinkles and the puffy skin underneath her dark brown eyes that easily told of the decades she had on me.

"How old are you, kid?"

The older woman turned her back to me as she reached for a single toilet paper roll that sat on the far end of a large, wooden shelf that was bolted to the cinderblock wall. A shelf that was identical to the one above my twin sized bunk, despite for its lack of belongings.

"Eighteen," I said.

The curly haired woman made a click with her tongue behind her teeth as she shook her head. "Barely legal and already locked up. Not a great start for you, huh?"

"No shit," I said.

I fidgeted as I noticed the amusement immediately drop from the woman's cheeks as she turned her body and lifted her brow up in reaction to my bitter tone.

"Sorry," I said with a low, remorseful voice.

I bit the inside of my cheek as she let me uncomfortably linger in a few seconds of silence while crossing her arms and shifting her weight to her back leg before she finally spoke. "Look, we all adjust differently in this place our first week. Just be careful who you take that temper out on in here, kid. The last thing you need is someone to kick your ass on the first day."

I nodded back with understanding to the warning tone that came off more helpful than threatening.

"I'm Sherman, by the way," my new roommate said as she pointed toward her chest.

"Max," I said looking down at my bare nails that had been stripped of their usual black polish.

"You got a last name, Max? Nobody goes by first names here."

"Evans."

"Welcome to the prison, Evans."

"Thanks," I said with a forced gratitude as I pivoted my legs around and lifted my feet onto the bed.

I fell back against the firm mattress and rolled onto my shoulder until I was facing the cinderblock wall. I closed my eyes to help avoid the scream threatening to rise in my throat before I allowed my mind to drift back to the only thing that had yet to be taken from me. My memories.

2

I walked sluggishly over to the line of inmates already waiting for their early bird dinner, subtly licking my lips as my mouth began to salivate. But my hunger shrunk with disappointment as my eyes followed the pair of gloved hands that were scooping out the unflattering brown, lumpy sludge.

I resisted the urge to grimace as I inevitably stepped up to grab my tray before turning to glance around the room in a subtle search for an empty seat. It wasn't but a few seconds of small steps forward before I met Sherman's welcoming glance, beckoning me over with a silent nod. I shrugged mostly to myself before I headed toward the empty stool across from my curly haired roommate.

"Hey," Sherman said.

"Hey," I said, noticing the four other pairs of eyes studying me as I lowered my tray onto the table.

"This must be her, right," a thin framed woman with a short blonde, pixie cut said. She was side glancing Sherman with a crooked smirk.

"Yep, this is my new roomie, Evans," Sherman said, glancing around at each pair of eyes.

"Welcome to hell, Evans. I'm Jones," the blonde said gesturing her thumb toward her chest before pointing across the table toward a heavy, middle-aged woman with short black hair that rested just below her ears. "That's Adams."

I caught Adams's unflirtatious wink before I turned my attention back to Jones as she introduced the two women on my right, near the end of the rectangle table. "And over there is Montgomery and Peterson."

Jones had said the names as if they were a package deal, only letting on which was which as she pointed toward the one sitting next to me first. My neck turned slightly to look at Montgomery, resisting the urge to let my eyes travel any further down than her slender neck, as I took in the high cheekbones of her youthful face that was surrounded by thick locks of long, chocolate brown hair.

The woman across from her had copper red hair that stood out against her pale, alabaster skin. The loose ponytail she had styled let me see the beginning forms of wrinkles in the creases around her baby blue eyes. Eyes that held enough of a possessive grimace to force me to swiftly look back across the table in time to catch Sherman's eye roll

"So, Evans," Montgomery said calling back my attention with a voice that felt just as seductive as her green eyes. "What are you in for?"

The longer I stared back at her piercing gaze and devilish smirk the more stumped I became. I was more curious to know what she had done and how she hadn't already talked her way out of it. She was a Venus flytrap and I needed to look away before she swallowed me whole. But once I turned my neck back around I noticed the rest of the table looking in silence, waiting for an answer, including my new roommate.

"Drugs," I said with a flat voice.

"Let me guess, they weren't yours, right," Adams said.

There was a chuckle around the table from everyone. Even Peterson joined in, despite her still untrusting stare. I understood where they were coming from. We were in prison after all. I'm sure everyone held a conviction to some extent that they were innocent. But how many of those people were telling the truth?

"Would it matter if I said no?"

I smiled humorlessly to the sound of laughter once again ringing out before looking down as I pushed the brown goulash around on my tray.

"You'll get used to it," Sherman said leaning in with a low voice.

I wasn't sure if that thought was a comfort or not. But it was certainly enough to keep me silent for the rest of dinner until I could finally escape back into my dorm-like cell.

"Drugs, huh?"

My body remained still on my mattress, only turning my neck to look over at Sherman as she made her way to the end of her bunk.

"So they say."

"I'm assuming it was possession, right," Sherman asked curiously.

"Something like that," I said softly while turning to look up at the ceiling as she undressed from her navy blue uniform into a pair of sweatpants and plain white t-shirt.

"How much were you holding?"

"I wasn't holding anything."

I turned my neck back to see my roommate tilting her head and pursing her lips as she narrowed her eyes. "How much were you charged with holding, then?"

"They counted over three hundred pills of ecstasy?"

"Wow," Sherman said with a nod of approval. "I underestimated you, kid."

"Nothing to be impressed about. They weren't mine."

My curly haired roommate twitched her eyebrows in amusement.

"Still sticking to that innocence?"

"If you mean the truth, then yes."

"Pills were always too juvenile for me—no offense," Sherman said while lifting her hands up apologetically.

I merely shrugged with indifference. "None taken."

"Heroin was always my weakness," Sherman volunteered.

"The only thing I've ever done is cigarettes."

Sherman lifted her eyebrows in surprise before falling onto her bunk.

"Well, they found themselves a smart one with you. You don't see it too often that the drug dealer is resisting the product."

"I'm not a drug dealer," I said with an irritated voice.

"No? So you just happened to be holding three hundred pills of ecstasy, randomly?"

"I wasn't selling anything."

"Oh," She paused with a nod before pointing toward me as if suddenly having an epiphany. "You're a mule. That makes more sense, with someone of your age."

I couldn't help grimacing at the comment. "What does that mean?"

"Just that it probably wasn't hard to convince a young, rebellious kid like you to carry drugs. You probably got more thrill out of it than your geometry class could satisfy."

"I'm not a fucking mule," I said.

"Well, not a very good one," Sherman said twitching her brow as she chuckled along with her teasing words.

"I wasn't—" I raised my voice, but stopped myself, defeated. It didn't matter what the truth was. Telling another inmate wasn't going to do me any good. It certainly hadn't done me any good at the trial.

"You got someone on the outside?"

I looked back at the ceiling, ignoring the change of subject as it only brought about more of a sting that I wasn't ready to handle.

"That's a yes. Are they the one who got you to carry those drugs you weren't muling?"

My head snapped back swiftly to the right. "She had nothing to do with it," I said with a venomous tone.

Sherman put her hands up in the air in surrender, resisting the pull of her lips as she sensed my discomfort. "Ah. So it's a she."

"Is that a problem?"

"Nope, I don't judge. I just owe Adams a Coke from commissary is all."

"Sorry for your loss," I said laying my hands on my stomach as I released a few short, controlled breaths.

"Can't win them all," Sherman said.

I let the silence linger a moment before I turned my eyes away from the ceiling and back to Sherman.

"What are you in for?"

"Drugs. Except I was definitely aware they were there," Sherman said with a teasing wink before turning over on her mattress.

"Night, Evans."

"Night, Ems," I said looking up at the ceiling with a dazed stare.

"What?"

The sound of Sherman's voice forced my mind to snap back to my present hell, turning my neck back to look over and see her confused squint.

"I said, goodnight."

I quickly rolled onto my shoulder to avoid any further inquisition of my slip, readily facing the cinderblock wall instead. But the one thing I couldn't escape was the same lingering depression that had begun to thicken in my veins as I thought about my new nightly routine. One down, three thousand forty-nine to go.

JANUARY 5, 2015
7:20 a.m.

I got onto the bus, reluctantly making my way toward one of the empty seats I saw near the middle right side.

"I see they started letting assholes on the bus."

I turned to see the familiar ocean blue eyes squinting back at me from across the aisle with a slight grimace as I took my seat. I couldn't ignore the small excitement that flipped my stomach at seeing the blonde again. I bit the inside of my cheek at the building fear that my new thrill had created.

"I'm new, so he doesn't know any better." I shrugged teasingly before winking at the blonde. "He'll learn soon enough. What about you?"

"Oh, well I'm not an asshole, so he had no problem letting me on," the blonde said in a tone that made it all too clear the excitement wasn't mutual despite her playful bantering words.

"Not driving the Mercedes today, Princess?"

"Not every princess has her own carriage."

I narrowed my eyes in disbelief until the blonde exhaled out her nose with surrender.

"Ok, fine. Maybe the carriage is in the shop. Happy?"

I remained silent but my smug grin said enough.

"Well, it's not a Mercedes it's a Mustang," the blonde said with a proud voice that was attempting to make a point.

"My mistake," I said, placing my hand to my chest with a mocking apology before leaning forward with a teasing grin. "No ride from the boyfriend, then?"

"No, miss know-it-all, my boyfriend couldn't because—" She stopped herself and looked around the bus shyly before she looked back over at my waiting, raised eyebrow. "Well…he just couldn't."

"How chivalrous," I said.

"I don't know why I even keep talking to you. You're so—"

"I'm so what?" I asked with a smug grin.

"Never mind," she said shaking her head before turning her gaze to look out the window.

"Don't leave me hanging; the suspense is killing me," I said.

Despite my fun, my smirk faded after a few minutes of unwanted silence. I couldn't help missing her voice and the cute way she got frustrated every time I teased her. Mostly, though, I couldn't help feeling the absence of those ocean blue eyes I was beginning to crave.

"I'm getting frostbite over here," I said.

Finally, the blonde turned her neck, squinting her eyes with confusion as she looked back up to meet my waiting gaze. "What?"

"You know, because of the cold shoulder you've been giving me," I said twitching my eyebrows.

Unfortunately, it was only enough to cause the blonde to roll her eyes in annoyance before turning her gaze back out the window. I sighed with disappointment as I resist the urge to reach out, clearing my throat to gain her attention instead.

"All right," I said in surrender. "I think we started off on the wrong foot."

"You think?"

"Look, I know I can be an asshole sometimes."

"Good to know you're aware of it," the blonde said without looking at me even though I could tell by the way her neck was turned she was waiting for me to continue.

"Well, I'm sorry if I hurt your feelings…"

My mouth opened to the invitation as my voice drifted off with anticipation. The blonde turned her neck back in my direction before lifting her gaze up to meet my peace offering grin. She chewed her bottom lip, letting the silence linger for a few seconds as if she was contemplating whether giving her name was a good idea or not.

"Emily."

"I'm sorry for being an asshole, Emily. Can we just...start over?"

"I guess," Emily said with a small shrug. "But only on one condition."

"Which is?"

"You tell me your name." Emily tilted her head while placing a piece of blonde hair behind her ear. "Unless you want me to keep calling you asshole."

"Max," I said with an amused smirk.

I lifted my hand out across the aisle just as the bus arrived at the school. Emily smiled warmly before reaching out to place her soft hand into mine.

"Nice to officially meet you, Max," Emily said releasing my hand, despite my disappointment, to shuffle out of her seat and head down the aisle to the front of the bus.

"You too," I said before lowering my voice and lifting my lips into a devilish smirk. "Princess."

"Asshole."

I stood with a new smile as I looked up to see Emily reveal a satisfied grin. I nodded while adjusting my backpack onto my shoulder, feeling as if these next six months wouldn't be so bad after all.

3

The reoccurring thoughts of the blonde that I had yet to see since getting off the bus were beginning to annoy me. I shook my head, opening up my spiral notebook, desperate for an artistic release and much-needed distraction. Unfortunately, as I dropped my hand to the paper, the silence was interrupted by a body dropping heavily into the seat in front of me.

"You must be the new girl."

"Yep," I said, continuing to draw without glancing up to meet the eyes of the deep-voiced boy.

"I'm Jason. Jason Bellman."

"Okay," I said with an apathetic tone.

"And you are—?"

"Not interested."

"You're a feisty one. I like that."

"I'm going to stop you right there," I said.

"Why's that?"

I rolled my eyes in frustration to his flirtatious tone and obtuse observation.

"So I don't have to hear you embarrass yourself anymore."

"Look at you already thinking about me," Jason said annoyingly tapping his finger on my desk to gain my attention. "So…are you going to tell me your name or should I wait for roll call?"

I sighed, reluctantly stilling my hand before I looked up to see a guy with brown hair that was gelled up on the top and cut short on the sides. But his full lips and dimpled, square chin were canceled out by the arrogance that radiated out of his hazel eyes. I groaned internally as he winked and began to circle his gaze around my face.

"Listen, buddy, you're barking up the wrong tree."

"What do you mean," Jason asked with a wrinkle forming between his thick eyebrows before the words registered. "Oh…oh!" His lips rose with stereotypical excitement as he leaned his elbows to rest on the edge of my desk. "You're into girls, huh?"

"Yep," I said with the pop of my lips.

His eyes narrowed before his gaze slowly made its way down to my chest with without much subtly. "Seriously, how is that possible?

"Well, you're doing a great job at reminding me why."

"You sure you just haven't met the right guy who knows what he's doing?"

"Oh my god," I said with a fake gasp as I clutched my chest. "I think you may be right."

"You know, if you want, I can help be that guy."

"Well, aren't you a gentleman," I said sarcastically.

"I can be gentle if you like," Jason said confidently.

I shook my head with a tight-lipped grimace. "I'll pass."

"You'll come around. They always do," Jason said before turning back around as the teacher called the class's attention.

"Those without brain cells, maybe," I mumbled.

I was all too thankful when history was over and I could escape into the hallway. At least that was until I reached my locker and noticed I had yet to shake Jason Bellman from my presence. Unlike my disappointment, the boy carried another satisfied grin when he noticed how close our assigned lockers had been. I was all too ready to make another quick exit when a bounce of blonde hair caught my attention from behind him.

"Hey babe, how was history?"

Jason gave me one final seductive wink before turning his body swiftly so that he could hold the blonde's face firmly. He leaned in to press his lips passionately against the girl's as if proving a point. But my stomach pulled inward, and my jaw involuntarily tensed once I finally took notice of the blonde attached to him.

"That good, I guess," Emily said with a surprised voice.

"Yeah. I can't wait to see where the semester goes," Jason said.

My stomach churned from the sight of their affection as Emily's ocean blue eyes suddenly found my stare.

"Oh, hey."

"Hey," I said.

Jason turned to look over his shoulder with confusion.

"You already know each other?"

There was an odd possessiveness to Jason's tone that didn't sit well with me.

"Yeah," I said. "Your girl's a real rebel."

"Who, Emily? I don't think so," Jason chuckled while Emily desperately tried to leave her gaze on her feet. "She's too uptight to be a rebel. But who cares when she's this hot, right?"

He smacked Emily's ass and cupped it with the same possession that caused her to jump slightly forward. The arrogance in his rhetorical question made it seem as if he thought it should be taken as a compliment. I couldn't help the desire to grab her wrist and pull her along with me while simultaneously wanting to punch Jason in the gut.

"You must be the chivalrous boyfriend who had more important things to do than pick up your hot girlfriend for school."

Emily's eyes snapped up to mine. I could see the grin she was resting on her lips as well as the blush beneath her cheeks before I looked back to see the irritated gaze of her boyfriend.

"I have to get to Spanish," Jason said.

Emily looked as if she was waiting for a kiss but Jason merely shut his locker and headed off down the hall. It didn't go unnoticed by either of us that he had swung his arm around the shoulder of some random short brunette, who giggled at the attention. I looked back to see anger and defeat form within Emily's blue eyes before she tried to shake it off once she noticed my attention.

"So that's the boyfriend, huh?"

"Don't start," Emily said as she turned and walked away.

MAY 19, 2015

The shaking beneath my body alerted me enough to open my eyes and instinctively swing my arm forward.

"Easy there, Rocky!"

I blinked a few times to adjust to the light of the cell, already feeling the bags that had formed underneath my eyes. I leaned on my left elbow as I used my other hand to wipe the sleep from the corners of my eyes.

"Sorry," I said with a deep raspy voice.

"It's cool, just thought I'd shut you up before the guards came around."

"Shut me up?"

"Yeah, I'd ask you who Emily was, but I have a feeling I already know."

My legs swung forward onto the floor as my body stiffened at the name coming from someone else's lips. I opened my mouth ready to say so many things, but all I could muster out was a simple, "Thanks."

"Sure," Sherman said. She took a few seconds to let the silence linger as if she was choosing her words carefully. "Hey, I know being here is a hard adjustment at first. Just give it some time."

I nodded with a tight-lipped grin that didn't quite reach my eyes despite my appreciation of her words.

"I'm going to get a shower before breakfast."

"See ya in a few, mule," Sherman said.

"I'm not a damn—" I stopped the useless defense as Sherman stood to leave the room, still chuckling as she walked down the hallway.

After my lukewarm shower, I leaned against the bathroom sink, taking in the bags underneath my eyes that showed the proof of my lack of sleep the night before. I was pressing the skin tenderly with my finger when I saw another body step in front of the mirror to my right.

"Rough night, Evans?"

My neck turned to see Montgomery standing with nothing but a towel wrapped around her tall, toned body. Her long wet hair cascaded down her back, leaving droplets of water on her firm skin as she began to rub lotion on her neck and shoulders. There was no denying she was a gorgeous woman.

"Didn't get much sleep," I said.

She continued moving her hands around her neck before flattening her palms slowly against her collarbones as she glanced over at me with a piercing gaze of seduction.

"I could help tire you out before bed if you want."

Her voice pulled me in like a siren as her lips curled up at the pull of my attention. There was a building lust that called me with the desire to take her against the sink as she purposely dropped her towel and moved over to leave only a mere few inches between our bodies.

Her full lips drew closer as if being pulled by another magnet that was attached to my own. But it was the stare of her emerald green eyes that finally shook me from my lustful daze. The lack of ocean blue was enough to make my body turn back to face the safety of the mirror without regret.

"Thanks for the offer, but I'll pass," I said

I ran my index fingers over my eyebrows, glancing sideways at her as she stepped backward with a smile before bending down to grab her towel from the floor.

"That's okay. I'm a patient woman, Evans," Montgomery said with another wink before heading out of the assigned bathroom.

I gripped the sink, dropping my head as I blew out a relieved sigh that Montgomery hadn't been more aggressive.

JANUARY 5, 2015
1:47 p.m.

I stepped up to the sink, reaching for a pump of soap as I heard the toilet flush from behind me. I rubbed my hands together under the warm water, letting my mind drift with the comfort.

"Fancy meeting you here."

My eyes snapped up to look up in the mirror in time to see Emily walking over to stand in front of the sink to my left. She was smiling at me with her cutely crinkled nose as she leaned over to lather her hands with the pink soap.

"Who knew our bladders would be in sync," I said.

She giggled while stepping back, grabbing a few paper towels to wipe her hands before attempting to toss them back into the trash, only to miss horribly.

"Well, that was embarrassing," I said, secretly finding it adorable as she blushed before bending over to pick them up. In the process, the hem of her sweater rose to expose the skin on her back. I couldn't help the stare her skin had pulled from me before I gave myself a mental slap to look away before she had stood back up in time to notice.

"I guess that's why I'm not on any sports teams," she said as she reached under the dispenser and politely handed me a paper towel of my own.

"Probably wise."

She playfully narrowed her eyes. "Isn't it rude to insult someone who just handed you a paper towel to wipe your hands?"

"I'm sure it is, but you just make it too easy."

Emily rolled her eyes before heading for the door. "You're welcome, asshole."

I winked causing her cheeks to lift as she tilted her head to the side with a small grin.

"Thanks, Princess."